WEEK END TO KILL

by FREDERICK NEBEL

SECRET CORRIDORS

by HUGH PENTECOST

WILDSIDE PRESS

www.wildsidepress.com

Published by Century Publications,
Printed in the United States of America

These stories are complete and unabridged. Characters and situations in these stories are fictional and any similarity to actual persons or places is purely coincidental.

WEEK-END TO KILL

By FREDERICK NEBEL

CHAPTER I

I HAD FINISHED packing and was waiting for the long-distance operator to ring me when Harrigan's trick auto horns struck three different trombone notes down in the street. He was a little early. The henna-colored roadster was parked at the curb with its canvas top snugged down in the slot and the rumble open. Harrigan was plumped comfortably behind the wheel. The sunlight gleamed on his bald pate, glanced off the blond and silver hair slicked back above his ears.

"In a couple of minutes," I called down.

He waved and nodded and said something but I didn't catch it because a Third Avenue El racketed past the foot of the block. The telephone rang and it was the long-distance operator saying she had my party now.

"Stan," I said, "this is Larry Webb."

"Oh, Larry. Hello. You're coming out, aren't you?"

"That's what I'm phoning about. I've been trying to get you since yesterday."

"We were out in the boat."

"Well, look. Do you remember Harrigan?"

"Harrigan?"

"I thought so. Listen, Stan. When you were in town the other night you invited me out and—"

"I know, sure. We're expecting you."

"Yes, but later in the evening you invited Harrigan too. He's a retired cop and runs a restaurant in West Forty-Eighth Street. We ate there. You and Harrigan got talking—"

"Oh, wait a minute. I know. Does he play ping-pong?"

"That's right. You asked him to come out with me and you'd take him on. But if it's not all right, I'll figure out a way—"

3

"Oh, no—nothing like that, Larry. It'll be swell."

"That's what I wanted to make sure about. Because Harrigan's a right guy and I don't want him to feel when he gets out there—"

"It's all right, I tell you. It's great. Ivy'll get a kick out of him and Vivian's here and there're some others—I don't think you know them—and I'm all for it. When will you start?"

"Any minute."

"Good. And Larry, I really want to see you. I—I want to get your advice—" He stopped short and if it was because of what I thought it was, it was somebody else listening in on an extension. "Well," he said, "I'll see you in a couple of hours, then. Remember, turn right just before you come to the bridge."

"Yes," I said. "You wrote the instructions down."

I carried my suitcase down two flights, through a vestibule, and out into Thirty-seventh Street.

Harrigan was standing on the curb leaning against the roadster's door. He wore a clay-colored sports jacket, a pale green shirt with a brown tie, tan gabardine slacks and a pair of brown reverse-calf shoes.

"Nice day for the country," he said.

He looked all right. His face was big, round, fat but not flabby, and in the very center of it, bunched neatly together, were small, bland eyes, a small nose, a small full-lipped mouth with upturned corners. It was a contented face; good-natured. His trunk was big, thick, broad, and his legs tapered away to rather small feet.

He took the bag away from me, and heaved it into the rumble. "How far is it, about?"

"Fifty-odd."

"Hour and a half."

"Two and a half, with traffic, Abe."

"I'll settle for two."

We drove over to the West Side express highway and north to the George Washington Bridge, where you come out on Riverside Drive. We went up Riverside Drive. We crossed the Hendrik Hudson Bridge and took the Sawmill River Parkway to the Cross County. We took the Hutchinson River Parkway to the White Plains-Port Chester road and at Port Chester we came onto the Boston Post Road.

Harrigan said, "This Mr. Cantwell, seems like a very nice and democratic gent. He used to work with you, didn't he?"

"Yes. On the 'Dispatch.' But his old man died and left him a lot of dough. Then he married Ivy Traynor. She was on the stage. His old man owned the Bridgepoint Metal Products and there were two sons and a daughter. Stan and Rupert, who's older, forty or so, and then Vivian's the youngest; she's twenty or twenty-one now. Stan's about my age, thirty; or he may be a year older. I haven't seen much of him in the past four years."

"He's a very democratic guy."

"He bought a newspaper a couple of years ago, but I don't think he works much at it. A guy named Mace Shelby runs the editorial end. Stan and Ivy are on the go a lot. Palm Beach. Hollywood. Bar Harbor. They just open this place a couple of months in the summertime."

"What was Mr. Cantwell talking about the South Seas?"

"He was just talking, I guess. He has a swell sister. I ran into her in Grand Central about two weeks ago but she was hurrying to make a train. Hadn't seen her in three or four years. She sure grew up."

"It wouldn't be her you're going to see, would it?"

"It could be. But I think Stan's okay too."

We turned under the New Haven tracks at Stamford and Harrigan said, "He looks like a guy you could feel sorry for. This stuff about the South Seas—"

"I guess I didn't pay much attention. He used to pull that when we worked on the 'Dispatch' together. Palm trees. White beaches. Coral reefs."

"Never did get there, huh?"

"No. Dough and then Ivy."

"Dough is what a guy uses to get places, ain't it?"

When we came within sight of the bridge I began giving directions We turned right toward the Sound and in a little while, about five minutes, caught sight of it through the trees, a live white metal flash in the sunlight. We passed between stone gateposts studded with chips of mica and followed a bluestone driveway upward among the evergreens. First we saw parts of the house, then we saw all of it—a square stone house with four white wooden columns out front.

There was nobody on the veranda but there were voices somewhere, outside, and the muffled smacking of a tennis ball. A houseman in a white coat came out and began burrowing in the rumble.

"Where's the garage?" Harrigan asked him.

"I'll put it away for you, sir."

"I'd rather put it away myself."

"Come on," I said. "It can wait. Let's see who's out back."

He shut off the switch, shoved the key in his pocket and we walked around the house.

On the east side of the house was a tile terrace with some wicker long chairs, two glass tables, some metal spring chairs. Glass doors were folded back, showing a pale blue floor inlaid with a dark blue anchor; a lacquered black bar with chromium and white-glass fittings.

"I hear people," Harrigan said, "but I don't see anybody."

There was a small veranda in back that looked out over a big lawn. Beyond the lawn an elaborate rock garden rose in tiers to a tennis court and to a pavilion with a glazed cement floor, rustic tables, a big glassed-in contraption that would play a lot of phonograph records one after another.

A man and a girl were playing tennis. The girl wore yellow shorts and a bandana halter, and her hair almost matched her shorts. She was not a good tennis player and the man was just kidding her.

"Who are they?" asked Harrigan.

I said I didn't know.

From the pavilion you saw the beach through a gap in the trees, but it was at least five hundred yards away.

The houseman was out back of the house removing a chair from a wooden crate.

"I'm going to like it here," Harrigan said. "Yes, Webby, I'm sure going to like it. I wonder where the ping-pong table is."

"Probably in the game room."

"I brought my own paddles. You take some guys, they like rubber. I like mine sanded."

We left the pavilion and went down the winding steps through the rock garden to the lawn. The houseman had got the chair out of the crate and was wiping it off. The chair was enameled green. We walked around to the tile terrace.

A girl was standing with her back toward us watching a Scottie chase a rubber ball. She had on a tailored white sun suit, the skirt of it pleated, and high-heeled white slippers. Her legs were long and very beautiful, and you could have fitted your hands around her waist. Her hair was copperish and like one big wave.

The Scottie got the ball and came racing back toward her, but at the last second he shot to one side and bolted between Harrigan and me.

"And with them short legs, too," Harrigan said.

Vivian said, "Larry Webb—Hello!"

"Hello, Vivian. Vivian, this is Abe Harrigan. This is Stan Cantwell's sister Vivian, Abe."

Harrigan said, "How do you do, pleased to meet you. I came up to play some ping-pong."

"Oh, good. That's what Stan said. He's on the boat but he'll be back any minute. The others are upstairs. Ivy, and Mabel Ryan and Roy Stockland. It's just great, Larry, having you out."

"We just got here."

"I'll bet you're thirsty. I'll ring—or if you'd rather mix your own, the bar's right there."

Harrigan raised his index finger. "Let me. What'll it be?"

"Just some vermouth. There's a chilled bottle in the icebox."

"You, Webby?"

"If there's any ale, ale."

"Yes, there's ale," said Vivian.

Harrigan nodded and went into the cool blue bar whistling "Time

On My Hands." There was no breeze moving but the air was mellow and not too warm. I stretched out in one of the wicker long chairs and put my hands behind my head.

"This is wonderful," I said. "Peace and quiet."

The Scottie gave Vivian the ball and she threw it away again and said, "Did you say peace and quiet?" She sat down and looked at me. "Larry, why did you come out here?"

"That's a nice question."

"No. I mean, why did you, Larry?"

"Swim. Lounge around. Maybe dance with you."

She stood up and held out her hand. "Come on."

"Not now, please. I don't like to dance till after the sun goes down."

She shook her head. "I mean I want to talk to you."

I got up and we strolled to the pavilion and sat down. They were still smacking the tennis ball back and forth and I asked, "Who's that?"

"Ivy's friends. George Hazelhurst and Karen Langard. She's a model. You see her in ads. George is in real estate and investments."

"He looks like a good tennis player."

"He's very fond of Karen. Honest, Larry, didn't Stan ask you out here for a special reason."

"If he did, he's been keeping it from me. He asked Harrigan out to play ping-pong."

Her forehead clouded and she shook her head. "He's not happy. He's —I don't know—he's desperately unhappy."

"Nobody's really happy. When I was a police reporter I wanted to be a sportswriter, and now that I'm a sportswriter, I'd like to do a column."

"But you're not really unhappy, Larry. Anyone can look at you and see that."

I leaned back. "You're looking swell, Vivian."

"It's just as though Stan were being driven by something inside him. Even when he's playing hard, having fun hard, I can feel it there."

George Hazelhurst and Karen Langard left the tennis court and ran down the slope. They went into the house.

I sat up and then stood up and said, "We'd better go back to the bar."

"Just don't let him do anything foolish, Larry."

"Listen, there's only one thing to do about a guy that's determined to be unhappy; let him alone. A lot of people around offering advice only makes him unhappier."

She stood up too. "All I asked was, did you come out here for a special reason."

"Well, I didn't."

"All right then."

CHAPTER II

HARRIGAN WAS leaning in the wide bar entrance drinking white stuff out of a tall, slender glass. He pointed with the glass to one of the tables. Vivian's vermouth was there and my bottle of ale alongside a tulip glass.

Vivian picked up her vermouth and smiled at him. Her body was very straight, each part flowing naturally and gracefully into the other. Her face was angular, with high cheekbones, a full forehead, deep violet eyes with soft smoky shadows beneath them. There was a flare to her nostrils and her upper lip was long. It was a passionate face but it made sense.

Harrigan lifted his glass, said, "Well, upsydaisy."

I had taken a mouthful of ale when the shot cracked and if the sound had been nearer, I'd probably have gagged. But it was far away, either inside the house or on the other side of the house. Harrigan really started more than I did. Vivian looked curious and bewildered as though she couldn't make out what it was or why it had occurred. We were both standing at the edge of the terrace and she turned and stepped to the ground and listened.

Harrigan was leaning comfortably again. He said off-hand, "That was a twenty-two."

"Some kids, probably," I said.

"Not just an ordinary twenty-two. Sounded like a super-X blast. Bad bullet for kids to use in the open. Too much range." He took a swallow of his eggnog. "Pretty close, too."

Vivian walked toward the back of the house, still listening, and then disappeared.

Harrigan said, "There ought to be a law against kids using them little guns. I shot myself in the foot when I was a kid. But you take these new super-X bullets, they're liable to bust the back out of the ordinary twenty-two rifle. Or them cheap revolvers they sell." He gestured with his glass. "That one might have come from a revolver or an automatic pistol. Brother, this sure is a good eggnog." He finished it, walked across the blue floor and washed out the glass back of the bar. Then he came out and said, "Guess I'll put the car away."

I crossed the bar and went into the living room. Two of the windows were open and I heard footfalls on the driveway and saw Vivian walk past. She was hurrying and in a minute was out of sight. I stood at one of the open windows and in a couple of minutes Harrigan drove past on his way to the garage.

When I turned around to go out, a tall, broad-shouldered man in a double-breasted white coat was standing in the entry-way from the main hall. I had the feeling that he had not just come there. He moved easily into the living room and said, "Hello. We haven't met, have we? My name is Stockland."

"Webb is mine. How do you do."

"Oh, yes. Stan said you were coming out. Did you just arrive?"

"About half an hour ago."

He looked straight at me and smiled, saying, "You must have made good time."

"Pretty good."

He offered me a cigarette and I took it. He had a soft, round voice with a lot of body to it, like good wine. His hair was coal black and fitted his chiseled head like a tight béret and his dark eyes were level without being blunt. He looked about forty.

I said, "Vivian's around outside somewhere. We were out on the terrace and heard a shot. Did you hear it?"

"Yes. It was probably off in the woods. Is Stan around?"

"Vivian said he was on the boat."

"You'll be around for a while?"

"Several days, I guess."

"Good," he said, and strolled toward the bar.

I walked to the entrance hall and went out to the front veranda. Vivian wasn't anywhere in sight. I followed the driveway down the west side of the house and saw Harrigan standing in front of a six-stall garage talking with a man in a chauffeur's uniform. The man was straightening a window screen that was warped in the middle.

Harrigan said, "This is Shultzy."

"How do you do, Mr. Webb," Shultz said. He was grimly preoccupied.

"The world," Harrigan said, "is a small place. Shultzy, for instance. He used to drive for the Department of Sanitation."

"Years ago," Shultz said defensively. "I been private for ten years."

"I was on the Broadway Squad then," Harrigan said. He placed his hand on Shultz's shoulder and smiled. "Still the same old Shultzy. You know, Webby, it near to busted his heart when he couldn't make the cops. He was always a cop at heart."

Shultz said, "An inch under height, was all," and moved off into the garage.

We strolled down the driveway. I heard the sound of an automobile motor droning uphill.

Harrigan said, "Some guy must have taken a cut at that with a niblick," and pointed to a raw gouge in the smooth lawn.

A beach wagon came up the driveway out of the trees.

"Did you see the kid with the gun, Abe?"

"Nope. Shultzy thinks it was some kid in the woods."

A hand waved at us from the driver's side of the beach wagon.

"This is Stan now, I guess."

"Handy things, them beach wagons," Harrigan said.

Somebody had brought our bags up and they stood in the center of a big corner bedroom. The rear windows looked toward the rock garden and the side ones were almost over the terrace. Harrigan tossed a coin. I called heads and it showed up tails, so I picked up my suitcase and carried it through the bathroom into a bedroom that was directly above the terrace. Harrigan came in and said:

"Leave your bathroom door open and I'll leave mine. Better circulation. There ain't a breath of breeze."

"You going to take a bath?"

"I took one this morning. I'll just freshen up. How would a Palm Beach suit go?"

"Anything I guess. It doesn't matter much."

"Say, that Mabel Ryan girl is sure hefty, ain't she?"

"She's a swimming teacher, I think."

"She was taking a snooze and didn't hear the shot. Miss Langard didn't hear it but she was taking a shower at the time, she says. So was Hazelhurst, he didn't hear it, either. The houseman and his wife, the cook, think it was in the woods, some kid hunting. The maid was running a vacuum cleaner and didn't hear it at all. Mr. Cantwell, of course, and that young guy Bennett weren't here. Mr. Cantwell's dead against guns and won't have 'em on the place. He says it was probably some kid in the woods. Well, no one's hurt; so what the devil."

I took a shower and was standing in my bathrobe, smoking a cigarette, when someone knocked. I said come in and it was Stan.

"Is everything all right?" he asked.

"Fine."

"I'm awfully glad you came out, Larry."

"It's a treat."

"Was I all right the other night?"

"You were high."

"I guess I was. Did I say anything?"

"Just the South Seas stuff."

"Did I say anything about Ivy?" He watched me closely.

"I don't think so. It was all about the South Seas and some schooner."

"Oh, that schooner. Yes. I can buy a ninety-footer, only two years old."

"I thought you had a boat."

"I have. But it's a fifty-four foot cruiser. No good for long hauls. This schooner would go anywhere."

"You're not really serious about this South Seas stuff?"

"Why not?"

WEEK-END TO KILL   11

I sat down and put on my socks. "Well, now that you ask me, I don't know. Maybe you're right."

He sat on the edge of the bed with his hands clasped between his knees. His eyes were light blue, dreamy, and wandered easily. His face was big and browned by the sun and his hair was light brown and thick and combed straight back from a widow's peak. He had big shoulders and big brown hands. He gave a sudden rueful laugh and stood up.

"Well, it's old stuff to you, Larry. I just wanted to make sure I didn't talk out of turn the other night. Come on down any time."

He went out and I finished dressing and stood by the window. The air was soft and sweet and summery. Ivy and Stockland were standing by the marble bird bath. I could see only his back, his square shoulders and lean head. They didn't seem to be saying anything. Downstairs in the bar the radio was playing.

Harrigan strolled in, looking very elegant in a white suit and a pale blue tie. He said, "Do you know what Shultzy said this afternoon?"

"No. What?"

"Well, I was saying what a nice, democratic gent I thought Mr. Cantwell was, and Shultzy says, 'Too damned nice for a lot of people I could name.' Just like that, like he was sore at somebody."

"Shultz looks like a sourpuss anyhow. You ready? Let's go down."

CHAPTER III

Ivy LOOKED AS if she had been born physically perfect, had remained so and would continue to remain so indefinitely. It was half fact and half illusion. Small tight brown waves of hair clung to her head. Her eyes were blue and as a rule wide open, and though this gave the impression of candor, it was misleading. She was not tall but when she stood alone you thought she was. She was very graceful.

It was almost ten and we were dancing in the pavilion to phonograph music. George Hazelhurst was dancing with Mabel Ryan and Stockland was dancing with Karen Langard. Vivian was dancing with a fellow named Norman Bennett who was the lifeguard at the beach club. Stan and Harrigan were sitting at a table talking.

Ivy said, "This is the first time I've had a chance to talk with you since you came."

"I've been around all the time."

"Tell me what you're doing."

"Don't you ever read the 'Dispatch'? Sports."

"I don't read sports. I think you once took me to a baseball game?"

"And you wondered why the man kept swinging at the ball all the time and never hit it. We went somewhere for dinner afterward and ran into Stan."

"We did, didn't we?"

"That was when you met him."

"I know."

"He'd been in the money about three or four months and you were the trader's half-caste daughter in that flop I can't remember the name of."

"*The Reef.*"

"Was that it? Anyhow, Stan saw it half a dozen times. Then it collapsed. The only part I remember was where you shot the Belgian pearl trader. By the way, did you hear a shot this afternoon?"

"I heard something. I thought it was a backfire."

"Maybe it was. Harrigan thought it was a twenty-two."

She turned her head and looked at Harrigan. "Where did you find him?"

"When I was first a police reporter in New York. He showed me the ropes. Stan invited him out to play ping-pong. He used to be a cop—plain clothes, when I knew him. Now he runs a swell restaurant."

"He makes a very good appearance."

"He was always a good dresser. Who's Stockland?"

"Roy? He's an architect. He designed this house. This is good rhythm, isn't it?"

We danced around once saying nothing. Then the music stopped and the houseman came out with fresh coffee and I went over and got some. Vivian came over too, a little flushed from dancing. It made her look lovely and fresh and buoyant.

I said, "If you can break away from the body beautiful sometime this evening, I'd like a dance."

"Is that nice."

"I hate guys with nice shapes. They show me up."

"Anyhow, you dance better. Really, Larry, it's wonderful having you out. It does Stan good. He was happiest, really, you know, when he worked on the 'Dispatch' with you. I'm sometimes sorry he ever quit."

"Show me a million and I'll quit any day."

Harrigan came over and poured a glass of water.

Vivian was looking around. "Where's Stan?"

"The houseman," Harrigan said, "come out and said something to him. He went in the house."

Ivy strolled over and asked idly, "Has Stan left us?"

"He went in the house a minute," Vivian said.

"I thought maybe he'd gone to bed again," Ivy said dryly.

Vivian colored. The others, all except Mabel Ryan, were busy talking among themselves. Mabel was staring at Ivy and there was the shadow of irony, not pleasant, around her mouth. Mabel was five-feet-ten, and well built. Her hair was flat brown, parted on the left, and her skin was deeply tanned. She had clear blue eyes, a wide generous mouth, a fine throat.

Vivian called out, "Let's have music, Roy."

Stockland had been looking curiously at Mabel Ryan. He came out of it suavely, saying, "Yes, of course, Vivian," and turned on the switch. For less than a minute Ivy's face looked beautifully sullen and her lips, usually a moderate red, looked rich and dark and hot. Then the music crashed and Harrigan, listening for a moment, said:

"You don't hear, many waltzes any more. Rumbas and tangoes and this screwy swing stuff. But no waltzes."

Vivian looked at me and let her breath out. There was anger in her eyes and it didn't go out of her as easily as her breath did. Ivy was dancing with Norman Bennett. Roy Stockland was watching the phonograph play.

"Dance, Vivian?" I said.

She said, "Love to," preoccupied, and I took her in my arms. I could feel her heart pounding in her breast and faint tremors traveling over her arms. I caught a glimpse of Ivy staring at me over Norman Bennett's shoulder with her wide-open, unrevealing eyes. We danced a couple of numbers and were starting on a third when Vivian said:

"I think Fritz wants me."

I stopped and watched her walk toward the houseman, who was standing on the pavilion steps. Mabel Ryan was watching her too. Vivian went away into the darkness with Fritz. She was way ahead of Fritz, hurrying. I poured some coffee and carried the cup over to the phonograph. Roy Stockland was still leaning on it watching the record go round.

He looked up at me, smiled. "Give up dancing?"

"Vivian went in the house. Fritz wanted her."

He glanced toward the house and then glanced around the pavilion. His face was remarkably clean cut and he looked as if he took good care of himself.

The music stopped and George Hazelhurst said, "Listen to the piano!"

Somewhere far away on the beach or on the water, someone was playing a piano. The notes came clear and liquid and I think the tune was "The Girl Friend." Everyone listened.

Harrigan said, "Nothing like a piano on the water."

"It's probably on the Aldebaran," Norman Bennett said. "There's a girl on board that can hit them."

We all listened. Somewhere in the house a door banged, an outside door. A minute later there was the sound of a raced automobile motor and then the harsh scuffing of tires getting away fast on the drive.

Karen Langard raised her arm in a mock-imperious gesture. She said, "Let us have music, Roy darling."

"She calls everybody darling," George Hazelhurst complained.

Mabel Ryan said, "Everybody calls everybody darling these days. It gets in your hair."

"Who calls you darling?" Ivy asked her.

"Okay, Ivy; you win," Mabel said.

I said, "Hello, Mabel darling."

"Thanks," she said.

Ivy looked at me and said, "I do believe we have a wit with us."

Harrigan laughed. "Who, Webby a wit? Webby?"

The music started again. Ivy turned her back on me and George Hazelhurst, grinning, was waiting for her. I sat down on the pavilion railing and after a couple of minutes swung over and dropped to the ground. The moonlight made the stones in the rock garden look pale gray and put a pale gray misty film on the lawn.

I went into the house through the bar and saw Stan slouched on a divan. His hair was mussed up. Vivian was sitting beside him and bathing his mouth with a wet cloth. There was blood on the cloth. Fritz was standing holding a basin of water and making gentle, concerned motions with his bony head. Vivian glanced at me but went back instantly to bathing Stan's mouth.

I sat down on the other side of him. He smiled and put his hand on my knee.

"Hello, Larry," he said.

Vivian said, "Don't talk now, Stan."

"Okay, Viv."

I watched her bathing his mouth. It wasn't bad, it looked as if just the lower lip was cut. It was more blood than anything.

"Alum will stop it," I said. "I've got a piece."

"I'll get it, sir," said Fritz, "if you'll—"

"No, I'll get it."

Stan said, "I may as well go up."

We went up and I got the alum and took it to Stan's bedroom. I said to him:

"You can probably hold it to your lip better yourself."

"Sure. Thanks."

I thought there were tears in his eyes.

"Is there anything I can do?" I asked.

"No. Just don't say anything to anybody. It'll be all right by morning. You go with Larry, Viv."

She kissed him on the cheek. "Good night, Stan."

He didn't want me to see the tears in his eyes, so he turned around and looked out the window.

I went downstairs with Vivian, saying, "He walked into something, didn't he?"

"A fist."

"What was he doing at the time, dreaming? I went three rounds with him once and he could sock--and take it, too."

"This was his brother Rupert. Stan just took it. He's taken a lot from Rupert." Her jaw grew firm. "He's taken a lot from too many people."

Ivy was in the downstairs hall. "Where's Stan?" she asked.

"Bed," said Vivian. "Sick headache." The color came up into her face again.

Ivy saw it and didn't say whatever she was going to say. Vivian walked swiftly past her toward the living room door. I leaned against the newel post. Ivy looked at me and I shrugged. At the door, Vivian stopped and turned and stared at Ivy and Ivy stared back at her and you could feel the tension—cold and bright on Ivy's part, hot and dark on Vivian's. Then Vivian went out.

Ivy's voice was unmoved: "What was it?"

"I don't know. Sick headache, I guess."

"You get funnier."

"All right. Why don't you go up and see?"

Her eyes shimmered coolly. She said, "Listen, Larry. Just because you once did a little necking with me, don't think you can come out to my house and clown all over the place." She swiveled and went out of the hall and I could hear her high heels pegging the living room carpet.

CHAPTER IV

THE BAR WAS empty. One light was burning: it was blue and cast very little radiance on the chromium fittings. I heard the phonograph playing and woven through the sound of the music was the singing of the tree toads.

It was dark back of the bar but I found the icebox and when I opened it a small light inside jumped on. A fat quart milk bottle was half full. I took it out, closed the icebox, poured the milk into a glass. The milk was cold and rich and tasted very good.

I hardly knew Rupert Cantwell. I'd seen him only once. In fact, I didn't know much about the family at all. I'd met Stan on the "Dispatch" and run around with him quite a bit the year he worked there. Vivian used to come into New York week-ends sometimes, and that was how I'd met her. I'd never met the old man and I guess the mother must have died years ago. Rupert, I believe, owned a great deal of stock in the company, but he was not active there; he had, Stan told me once, political ambitions. He was the gregarious type, a bit flamboyant as I remembered him. Maybe a little hot-headed.

From where I was leaning against the back of the bar I could see part of the living room. Fritz appeared in that part, closed the French doors on the west side. He emptied some ashtrays. There were other footsteps and Fritz looked up and then went on with what he was doing. Shultz appeared in the part of the room that was visible to me.

"I don't see the boss around outside. Is he upstairs?"

Fritz didn't stop what he was doing. "Yes," he said.

"I've been trying to get him alone," Shultz said grimly. "I think I'll go up. I got something to tell him."

Fritz stopped and shook his head. "No. He's turned in. He don't feel good. Don't you go up."

"Who was that got away in that car so fast?"

Fritz shrugged. "Why don't you mind your own business, Oscar?"

"You know," Shultz said, folding his short strong arms, "I feel like chucking this job."

"Jobs are easy to find, I suppose."

"No, they ain't. But I get things on my mind and I can't get them off. You see, Fritz, all the time I was a kid I wanted to be a cop. I tried and tried. It was in me, the thing that makes a cop. I keep putting two and two together all the time."

Fritz looked at him curiously. "What are you talking about?"

"Nothing," Shultz said, unfolding his arms, sliding his square hands into his coat pockets. "It wouldn't do you any good to know anyhow. It don't do me any good. It just makes me think and figure and I get sore."

"Look, Oscar," Fritz said, "the less you know, the better it is. Hear nothing, see nothing, say nothing."

"Well, *you* ain't ever heard me say anything."

"How's the new sport shoes you got yesterday?"

"They kind of hurt," Shultz said, looking down at his feet. "But I'm wearing 'em, anyhow. Well, I'm going out. Probably be back late." He left the room and in another minute Fritz left also.

The music in the pavilion hadn't started again and the bar, with the soft blue light, was very restful. I suddenly felt like smoking a pipe.

As I reached the top of the staircase I heard a radio playing very softly. It sounded as if it came from Stan's room. I knocked on his door.

He opened it and said, "Oh, Larry. Come in."

"I heard the radio."

There was no blood on his lip but there was a small lump that looked like a small onion. He was in trousers and undershirt and held a big map in his hand. On a small desk were some more maps.

He said, "I'm afraid you're not having"—he gave a little apologetic laugh—"a very good time."

"I'm having a swell time."

"I've always envied the easy way you take things, Larry."

I stopped at the desk and glanced at the maps.

"You'll laugh," he said.

"Why?"

"Oh, those maps. I like to look at maps. I can almost picture myself in the places the maps show."

I sat down in an armchair and said: "What you ought to do, you ought to see what those places look like."

His voice was low, an eager whisper. "I'd like to! There's nothing in the world I'd like to do more." He sat down on the edge of the bed. "But it just can't be done."

"This newspaper cramp your style?"

He shook his head. "No. I've got men running it that know a hundred times more than I do about it." He rubbed his hands together slowly. "The paper would be in good hands. Shelby's a crack editor. I don't interfere with him."

"If you did, he'd probably quit."

"I hadn't thought of that. But I just don't interfere with him. That's what's causing this trouble between Rupert and me. Rupert wants me to put the rein on him but I told him, no, I won't do it." He touched his lip. "Rupert loses his temper sometimes."

"Who's Shelby after?"

"The district attorney's office and a couple of magistrates. He's hammering the state capital for a special grand jury. It happens that Rupert and Stahlman, the district attorney, are old classmates, lodge brothers, and if he plays along with Stahlman and that crowd he'll probably be senator in a couple of years. He gets incensed when I tell him I signed a contract with Shelby. Of course, I could let Shelby go and pay him for the remainder of his term of contract, but I feel he knows what he's doing, and he's doing right. Rupert says I'm all wrong, Ivy wants me to lay off, Vivian's frightened, George Hazelhurst says that we'll never get a special grand jury with the political set-up, and Roy Stockland just thinks I'm a plain fool." He slapped his knees. "I sometimes wish I'd never bought the paper. But I bought it and I believe in Shelby and I won't interfere with him."

"What's Vivian frightened of?"

"Oh, some bit of nonsense." He pulled open a desk drawer, rummaged in it, drew out a sheet of wrapping paper about ten inches square. Pasted to it were letters clipped singly from a newspaper but arranged to read: LAY OFF OR ELSE!

I said, "Who was it sent to, you or Shelby?"

"Me." He shrugged. "It doesn't really mean anything. Some crank, probably."

"Cranks shoot kings and dictators and presidents."

"But what could you do about a thing like that? Obviously no one in the district attorney's office would be stupid enough to pull that hokum."

I threw it on the desk. "No. Probably some guy way down the line that feels patriotic. Or somebody, not necessarily a politician, who might get roped in if a special grand jury sat. Did Shelby get anything?"

"A phone call yesterday from a fellow with a very thick lisp. 'Cut out this special grand jury stuff,' he said, 'or you'll be sorry.' Another crank. You can't get anywhere, do anything, on this crank stuff. You don't even print it, Larry."

"Well, you're right about that. But I'd be careful."

"But you wouldn't let stuff like this make you ease up, would you?"

"No. But I'd be careful. You never know what some of these screw-balls will do. You ought to buy that schooner and take that trip. Let Shelby fight it out. He started it."

He stood beside the desk, gazed down at the map, and said, "Pago Pago. What a name! Pago Pago! And Samoa! And Fiji!"

"Take Ivy with you."

His fingers were splayed stiff above the map. Gradually they relaxed, curled up. I saw him swallow. We were silent for a couple of minutes and then I got up and walked to the door. As I put my hand on the knob, there was a knock. I opened the door and saw Mabel Ryan. She laughed good-humoredly.

"Come in," I said.

"No, I just wanted to see how Stan was. Hello, Stan."

"Hello, Mabel. I'll be all right by morning."

"We're all going to Jonesy's for steak sandwiches. You going, Larry?"

"Sure. I'll be along in a minute."

She walked down the corridor. Her back and shoulders were golden-brown against the color of the blue dress she wore. Just before she turned the corner she looked over her shoulder and smiled.

Stan said, "Mabel's a grand kid. You ought to see her handle a boat."

"I'll bet."

"Got a heart big as a house."

He came over and laid his hand on my shoulder. "Go along, Larry. Have fun."

"I really could go for a steak sandwich right now. See you in the morning."

CHAPTER V

WE DIDN'T GO to Jonesy's after all. Norman Bennett said there was a new orchestra at the beach club, so we drove to the beach club. It was pretty crowded. Karen gave a squeal of delight and ran up to the orchestra leader. He inclined his head toward her and they talked while he kept his baton moving. When the music stopped she brought him over to the table and said:

"Ivy, this is Jack Kingsley. Jack, my hostess, Ivy Cantwell. You can just call everybody else darling."

He nodded to Ivy, grinned at the rest of us, looked for an extra minute at George Hazelhurst. He was a square-built man, with conical shoulders and a large, dark amiable face. But he said he couldn't stop, patted Karen's shoulder and strode back to the orchestra.

Karen said, "I met him in Miami when he was playing at the Everglades Casino. He's really awfully nice."

"Very democratic," Harrigan said.

"Yes," Karen nodded. "Jack lost a lot of money in Miami. Something or other—I forget. He's very attractive, don't you think?"

Ivy said, "We ought to ask him over to the house."

"He's a divine piano player."

Norman Bennett said, "Maybe George would disapprove. I think Karen has a yen for this guy."

Karen rolled her eyes, said, "H-m-m-m!"

"Trouble is," Norman Bennett said, "George is stodgy. All real-estate brokers are stodgy. He's a good tennis player but he's stodgy."

Harrigan said, "Do you play ping-pong, Mr. Hazelhurst?"

"No."

"Stodgy," said Norman Bennett. "Doesn't play ping-pong. Georgie-porgie does *not* play ping-pong."

"You're tight," George Hazelhurst said.

"Don't get mad, George." Norman Bennett laughed.

Vivian said, "He's not mad, he's just preoccupied."

"If you people insist on discussing me," Hazelhurst said, "maybe I ought to leave the room."

Norman Bennett held up his hand. "See? George is mad. I did it. I apologize, George."

"All right, all right. I accept your apology."

Mabel said, "Good. Now let's have Welsh rabbit."

We all had Welsh rabbit. At midnight there was an intermission in the dancing and Harrigan, after a short talk with the headwaiter, went back to inspect the kitchen. I went out to the veranda with Mabel Ryan for a smoke. The breeze coming in off the Sound was stronger now and you could see the white surf breaking on the beach.

"Too bad Stan's not along," I said.

"I suppose you thought it was funny when I knocked at his door."

"Who, me?"

"I've known Stan since I was a kid. We used to sail a lot together. He had a little sailboat and we'd go out and I learned to handle it just as well as he did."

"Of course, I only met him when he came to New York to work on the 'Dispatch.' "

"He hasn't changed a bit," she said. "All that money, and he hasn't changed a bit." She was sitting on the veranda rail swinging her legs. "Sometimes I think it might be better if he did. Better for himself. Things and people have a habit of getting in his way. People take advantage of him. I get so mad sometimes that I could—" She shrugged. "But I guess you know him pretty well too. Did he ever show you his maps?"

"I saw them tonight."

She leaned back against a pillar. "That's what I mean. He hasn't changed a bit. We used to pore over them together."

"I told him tonight; I said, 'Why don't you buy that schooner and see what those places are like?' "

She sat up and gave a short laugh. "Don't be silly."

Hard footfalls came up from the dark end of the veranda and George Hazelhurst strode past without seeing us. His hands were clenched. His jaw was knotted. In his eyes was a blind headlong look and there were ragged red patches high on his cheeks. I caught the flick of his coat-tails as he swung inside.

Mabel said, "George looks mad enough to hit a cop."

"Does Bennett always ride him?"

"Norman doesn't like him."

"Why?"

"Oh, no reason. He just doesn't like him. You know, you just meet a person sometimes and you don't like him. There doesn't have to be any reason. Norman's sweet on Vivian."

"That's what I thought."

"George was making quite a play for Vivian but she didn't give him any encouragement. Then Karen Langard turned up. He's either nuts about Karen now or he's trying to get Vivian sore. Here comes your friend."

Harrigan came strolling down from the dark end of the veranda.

"I just been back in the kitchen," he said, stopping. "They got a nice one. Not as modern as mine, though. When you come to New York, Miss Ryan, you ought to stop by my place. Try my turkey under glass."

"Do you do your own cooking?"

"No. I got a French chef. But I've always been interested in recipes. My Viennese Potpourri is my own. And"—he leaned closer—"I can give you a better Welsh rabbit than they dished out here tonight."

"Who gave it such a swell name?"

"What, the Viennese Potpourri? Webby, here. I used to call it Harrigan Stew. Come on. Where's the bunch?"

When the music started again we all came together at the table and Norman Bennett grabbed Vivian and trotted her out onto the dance floor. Harrigan bowed before Ivy and was very stately about leading her out. Roy Stockland raised his eyebrows at Mabel Ryan and they went out. I waited a while to see if George Hazelhurst was going to dance with Karen Langard, and when he showed no signs I asked her to dance and she sparkled. Hazelhurst remained at the table, his lean face stony.

Karen Langard said, "George is certainly determined to enjoy himself. I am fond of him, though."

"You practically fell all over that orchestra leader."

"Oh, don't—now don't, please, pick on me. It was just that I was overjoyed to see Jack. He's sweet. But goodness, Jack's married and has two kids and he *adores* his wife."

But Hazelhurst wouldn't pull out of it and we all decided to go home at one. Norman Bennett didn't go with us because he lived in one of the club cottages and had no car. Out in the parking lot, he kissed Vivian good night. I was already seated in the back of the phaeton and by the time everybody else got in, it was pretty crowded. Mabel had to sit on Harrigan's knees and Vivian sat on mine. Roy Stockland drove.

Vivian twisted around and said, "Have a good time, Larry?"

"Swell."

"It was sure the nuts," said Harrigan.

Roy Stockland was opening up the phaeton.

"Not so fast," Karen Langard said. "There's no fire, Roy."

He eased up on the throttle but made no comment.

Vivian leaned back against me. The wind blew her hair against my face. I had no place to put my hands so I put them around her waist. Next to me, George Hazelhurst was stiff, silent.

Karen Langard said, "Please, Roy, not so fast."

He eased up again on the throttle. "Sorry, Karen."

Harrigan said, "Let's sing. Let's all sing something."

Vivian moved her head. "My hair's blowing in your face," she said.

I said, "Let it. I like it."

"I thought you like to dance with me too."

"Sure. So does Bennett, and he's quicker on the trigger."

Roy Stockland was speeding again.

CHAPTER VI

HARRIGAN MADE a great deal of noise scrubbing his teeth. He was wearing red and black striped pajamas and a blue robe. White braid formed his initials on the breast pocket of the robe.

I was leaning in the bathroom doorway drinking a glass of ice water. "You're too dressed up for bed, Abe," I said.

He didn't answer but smacked his big freckled hands together and began whistling "Time On My Hands."

"Now for a little reading," he said, "and then sleep, sweet sleep. I sure had a swell time tonight, Webby. Nothing like the country." He strode to one of his bedroom windows, braced his arms on the sill, inhaled deeply. "Ah, you can't beat it. It's wonderful."

He poured ice water from a thermos pitcher into a glass and sat down on the edge of his bed. He drank and he looked at me several times, curious, half-smiling.

"You don't know any of these people, do you Webby?"

"Only the Cantwells."

"That's what I mean. They all sure razz each other, don't they?"

"It's all in fun."

"Yeah, I guess so. But for a time there tonight I sure thought Hazelhurst might take a poke at that kid Bennett. What do you think of Hazelhurst?"

"I don't know. What should I think?"

"I mean, he don't take a kidding."

"Did you try kidding him tonight?"

"Me? No. When?"

"During the intermission at the club."

Harrigan gave a bland look. He shook his head. "Nope. I guess it was that band leader Kingsley. Kidding or something. I went back to the kitchen to look it over and when I left, I left the back way, to get a breath of air. Hazelhurst and this band leader were standing in the driveway near the end of the veranda. I don't know what they were saying."

"I think Kingsley knows him."

"Yeah. I caught that look at the table too." He drained the glass, set it down, kicked off his slippers. "Well, baby, pick up your toys and go to your own room." He got under the covers, put on his glasses, picked up the book. "What about breakfast?"

"Any time, up here or downstairs, Vivian said. There's a buzzer back of your bed."

"What kind of bird's that?"

"It's a whip-poor-will."

I went to bed and lay in the darkness listening to the whip-poor-will. The glow from Harrigan's bed light shone faintly on the open bathroom door. In about fifteen minutes his light went out and I heard him sigh contentedly. It must have been almost two o'clock.

A gentle rhythmic shoving on my shoulder woke me up but not completely and it was Vivian's voice saying, "Larry—sh—it's Vivian, Larry," that made me open my eyes. It was dark, there was no moon any longer, and waking up in a strange bed in a strange house, it took me a minute to get things straight. "It's Vivian, Larry," she began again in a reassuring whisper. "Sh!" And then she waited, probably to me a chance to come around completely. I sat up and my chest and head felt heavy from having been so hard and fast asleep. The sound of Harrigan's snoring came into my room.

Vivian whispered, "I'd better close that door." I didn't hear her close it but I knew she had because the sound of Harrigan's snoring almost vanished. I pulled on the reading light clipped to the head of my bed.

She came back and sat on the edge of the bed. "Stan's not in his room," she whispered. She was wearing a turquoise silk robe trimmed with old lace. There was no make-up on her lips and they looked pink, like pink coral.

"I heard a sound, something fall," she said, "and I got up—my room's across the corridor from his—and looked in his room. It was Kilts."

"It was what?"

"Kilts. The Scottie. He sleeps on Stan's bed and sometimes he dreams and falls off. He fell off. Stan wasn't in his room."

"Maybe he went downstairs for something."

"The bed wasn't slept in."

I was having an awful time waking up. "Did you look downstairs?" I asked.

"No, I didn't."

"Well, look downstairs, why don't you?"

"Wait here. I'll be back," she said.

She left the room, closing the door without a sound. I got out of bed, poured some ice water from the thermos bottle·into the palm of my hand and then splashed it in my face. Then I put on my bathrobe and slippers. Vivian came back in a couple of minutes.

"No," she said. "Everything's dark."

"He probably went out somewhere. Did you look in his room when we all came home?"

"No."

"Maybe he got lonesome and went out."

Her face was white, her eyes very round. She whispered, "I didn't tell you about the threat he received the other day."

"He did. I don't think it means anything."

She pressed her hands together. "We shouldn't have left him alone."

"There were servants in the house, weren't there?"

She nodded. "Yes. Fritz and his wife Emma and the maid Lily. Oscar has quarters in the garage."

"Why don't you ask Fritz if he went out while we were all gone? I'll go to Stan's room."

"All right."

She had left the light burning in Stan's room and when I looked in Kilts raised his head and gave a low growl.

"Nice Kilts," I said. "Nice Kiltsy."

The room looked the same as when I'd last been in it. The maps were still on the knee-hole desk. The clock on the desk said four.

Vivian came in and shook her head. "No, Fritz didn't hear or see him go out."

"How late was Fritz up?"

"Till midnight, he said."

I said, "You can see the room's all right. He probably took the car and went out."

"The roadster and the sedan were in the garage when we all came home in the phaeton. And Oscar was out in the beach wagon. Mr. Harrigan's car was in and so was George Hazelhurst's and Roy Stockland's. Stan would've had to walk."

"Are all the cars still there?"

"I asked Fritz to look. He said yes."

I looked around the room. "Well, I'll bet there's nothing wrong. I'll bet you'll find he went somewhere somehow. Go to bed. Wait till morning." I went to the door. "I'll see you in the morning."

She was staring vacantly at Stan's desk.

"All right. Kilts. Here, Kilts."

We all moved into the corridor and then Vivian pushed open the door to her bedroom. She motioned to the Scottie and he went in, his rear end waddling leisurely. I stood and waited until she had gone in also, then I walked slowly and quietly to my room.

I was in bed about five minutes when I heard a door close somewhere on the same floor and not far from mine. Not far enough away for it to have been Vivian's door, or Stan's, or Ivy's. It could have been Roy Stockland's, Karen Langard's, George Hazelhurst's, Mabel Ryan's. Or it could have been Harrigan's. I was too sleepy to get up and see, or even to wonder much about it.

CHAPTER VII

WHEN I GOT up at half-past nine Harrigan was having breakfast in bed.

"Good morning, Webby," he said. "Between me and you, I don't think it's so hot."

"What isn't?"

"Breakfast in bed. It's too damned roundabout. First I get up and take a shower and wash my teeth and gargle and then I get back in bed again. Well, it don't hurt to try anything once. Want some coffee?"

I got a glass and poured hot coffee into it from a thermos pot. There was a rumpled newspaper on the bed.

"What's in the news?"

"The Dodgers won a ballgame."

"What did the Giants do?"

He looked smug. "Hubbell pitched." He held up three fingers. "Three hits." He squinted at me. "You look dopey, Webby. What's the matter, didn't you sleep good?"

"I always wake up slow."

The coffee was taking hold, however, and by the time I had showered and dressed I felt all right. When I went downstairs George Hazelhurst was eating breakfast alone on the terrace.

"Nice day," I said.

"Peach."

"Do you mind if I join you in some breakfast?"

"Sit down, sure."

I pressed the buzzer in the bar and when Fritz came out I told him what I wanted. I asked, "Has Mr. Cantwell eaten yet?"

"Yes, sir."

The sun was warm and it felt good on the back of my neck. I was practically completely awake and really hungry now.

Hazelhurst said, "Would you like part of my paper?"

"No, thanks. But you go ahead and read."

"I understand you work on a newspaper."

"Yes. That's how I met Stan."

He gave a short, amused laugh. "Stan's a babe in arms when it comes to newspapers. He still believes in the power of the press."

"I guess it's overrated."

"This fellow Shelby, Stan's editor, is an exhibitionist. He's trying to fight a tight political machine."

"Well, there's no harm in trying. Someone has to start things."

Hazelhurst gave me a look of disapproval. "If you had a brother aligned with a political group, would you go out of your way to castigate that group?"

"I don't think it's as cut and dried as that. The way I understand it, Stan signed a contract with Shelby giving him free editorial rein. What's stopping Rupert from breaking off any connection he has with this group?"

Hazelhurst leaned across the table and said, "Listen, you don't know Shelby. He's an egotist. A rat."

"Well, an egotist maybe. But no rat."

"You don't know him."

"Sure I do. I worked two years under him. I think he's a great guy."

Hazelhurst's face grew red all over. He gave a jerky little laugh. "Well, I'm sorry. I didn't know—I wouldn't have—I didn't mean to—"

"Think nothing of it," I said.

"I'm really very sorry."

"Sure. Sure."

Fritz brought my breakfast and after a couple of minutes Hazelhurst excused himself and went into the house. He was very slender and lithe and sun-browned and I guessed he was quick-tempered. You got the feeling that all his nerves were very close to the surface and that he was pretty touchy.

As I was finishing breakfast Vivian came out, her step quick and springy.

"Morning, Larry."

"So you busted up my sleep for nothing. Go away."

"I guess it was stupid of me. He'd gone to the boat. He couldn't remember whether he'd locked up, so he walked over, it's only half a mile. Then he decided to sleep there. He walked back this morning."

"How is his lip?"

"Pretty good. Everything seems better in the morning. Stan says we'll all go for a sail today and have a late luncheon on the boat—out somewhere. Don't you think that will be nice?"

"I'm all for it. Anything. I'm on a vacation. Does Norman Bennett have to go?"

"He can't. He's on the beach till five."

"I'm glad to hear it."

"Oh, Larry, Norman's all right, he's all right."

"You ought to consider the lackadaisical type. It makes a better house pet."

"I like the lackadaisical type too, Larry."

I said, "I think the maid wants to see you." The maid had come to the edge of the bar and was standing there.

"Excuse me, Miss Cantwell," she said.

Vivian said, "Yes, Lily?"

"I took your breakfast to your room. Should I bring it down here?"

"No, Lily. I'll go up."

When Vivian had gone I wandered across the lawn to the garden. I was standing there when a black sedan pulled up out front. Two men were in it and one remained at the wheel while the other got out and looked at the house.

The man at the wheel said something to him and he looked from the house to me and then came over. In his hand he carried a hard straw hat.

"Good morning," he said. "Are you Mr. Cantwell?"

"Good morning," I said. "No, I'm not. Do you want to see Mr. Cantwell?"

He nodded. "Yes, I'd like to."

We went over to the terrace and I said, "Have a seat," and pressed the buzzer in the bar. He sat down and laid his hat upside down on another chair. He looked about thirty-five and was of middle height and wore a double-breasted gray suit and brown oxfords. His hair was black and bushy and so were his eyebrows. His skin was naturally dark.

Fritz appeared and said, "Yes, sir?"

"This man wants to see Mr. Cantwell," I said.

Fritz looked at him, raised his eyebrows. "Who should I say is calling?"

"Police. Pascarella."

"Yes, sir."

Fritz hurried.

Pascarella said, "That's a nice garden. I've had a lot of trouble with my zinnias this year. Those out there are nice, ain't they?"

"I don't know much about flowers," I said.

"Nice," he said, tipping back in his chair, rocking it gently. "Nice calendulas too. I've had a lot of luck with calendulas."

Stan's sneakers made a flat rubbery slapping sound on the bar tiles. His eyes were bright, curious.

"Morning, Larry."

Pascarella stood up. "Mr. Cantwell?"

"Yes. How do you do."

"I guess I got some bad news for you." Pascarella squinted at a small printed form he held in his hand. "Oscar G. Shultz. Worked for you, didn't he?"

"Yes. Yes, of course. My chauffeur."

"We found him dead in your station wagon this morning. About a mile from here. On the river road."

Harrigan sighed and said, "Well, here today and gone tomorrow. Yup. Poor Shultzy. A guy never knows, does he?"

He was sitting on a chair in Shultz's room in the garage with his hands hanging between his knees. Pascarella was going through the dresser drawers and Engle, his partner, was reading a batch of old letters. Engle was younger than Pascarella. He wore a tweed lounge suit and there was a yellow cowlick that stood up at the crown of his head.

"Nope," said Engle, snapping a rubber band around the batch of letters, "There's nothing in these to hang a hat on. I think we're going to find that Shultz probably gave some guy a lift and the guy let him have it."

"Probably," Pascarella said.

Harrigan asked, "Did you find any dough on Shultzy?"

Pascarella, closing a dresser drawer, shook his head. "Just some change. Sixty cents. Whether he had anything in his wallet, I wouldn't know. There was just his driver's license in it. It was on the seat. I sent it with the other stuff to the lab, for fingerprints. We ought to get some off the car too. But that don't say it'll get us anywhere."

"Where does that river road go?"

"It hits the state highway about two miles up. People off the boats use it most. That's why I don't think it was some bum thumbing his way across the state. I think maybe it was some local guy. A transient'd stick to the state highway. But I don't know why he should've taken the ignition key."

Harrigan said, "What did Shultzy get hit with?"

"I don't know. There were no tools out in the wagon and when we found the kit under the seat it was all complete. He was probably socked with a gun butt. It stands to reason. Look. The beach wagon when we found it was about twenty-five feet off the road back of a gravel heap the city keeps there for the road. It's my guess the guy pulled a gun on him and made him drive there, then clouted him over the head. The only other thing would be that he parked there with a girl and she did it. I don't know."

"Tell 'em what else," Engle said.

"What else what?"

"The shoes."

"Oh, yeah; the shoes," Pascarella said. "He was in his socks when we found him. No shoes. No shoes anywhere."

Harrigan said, "That'd kind of indicate it was some tramp after all. A guy that needed shoes to walk in. Were there any footprints around in the gravel?"

"Sure. They went straight from the wagon to the road. You can't follow them on a black-top road, though. I got a man out from headquarters to preserve two impressions, right foot and left." He turned to Engle. "Find anything?"

"Nope."

"I didn't think we would. Listen, Joe, go and ask the help if they got any idea where he went last night. If they haven't, ask 'em if they know any places he was in the habit of going. Ask 'em if they know what time he went out."

"Okay, Al."

Engle went out.

Harrigan said, "No shoes at all, huh? If he took Shultzy's shoes, what about his own? You didn't find them, huh?"

"No shoes at all," Pascarella said morosely.

Harrigan picked up one of a pair of white sports shoes and looked inside it. He said, "Size eight." He placed the shoe back on the floor beside its mate and said, "Of course, there's no explaining the things some guys do. He might have reached out to shut the ignition switch and stuck the key in his pocket right then." He scratched his jaw with his thumbnail. "On the other hand, maybe it was a woman."

Pascarella said, "You mean she put his shoes on and carried her own, to make it look like it was a man?"

"Something like that. But then Shultzy was no cripple. She'd had to be a pretty able-bodied female."

"Listen, judging from some of the janes I been running across lately, they're plenty tough enough."

Engle returned and said, "The butler or whatever he is, this man Fritz, says Shultz said he was going over to the amusement park on the beach. He went out in the wagon about eleven."

Pascarella shook his head. "If he went to the amusement park, what was he doing a mile from here up the river road? If he drove home from the park, he'd hit here without being on the river road."

"How do I know?" said Engle. "I'm just telling you what the guy told me."

"Of course," said Pascarella, "he could have picked up the party between here and the park and the party could have made him drive past here to the gravel pit. Anyhow, he probably didn't go to the park at all. He probably changed his mind and went into town. The river road would be a short cut home from town. Anything else?"

"Well, I heard he used to go in town and kill a lot of time at a bar called Dowd's, in Prince Street. You know, Dowd's Bar and Grill. And then the maid said he used to talk about the Gingham Inn, that roadhouse on the Post Road."

"How about the amusement park?"

"They said he liked the Beer Barrel."

"How about women?"

Engle shook his head. "He probably kept that to himself."

"Okay." Pascarella looked around the room. "I guess there's nothing here. Pleased to meet you, Harrigan. I'll be back and forth here a couple of times, I guess. Routine stuff. Come into headquarters sometime and meet the gang."

"Sure," said Harrigan. "That's a swell idea."

Pascarella stepped down to the narrow bluestone walk outside the door. Engle joined him and they wandered down the driveway. Harrigan stood in the doorway watching them. After a couple of minutes he turned and said:

"What's the matter, Webby, d'you lose your tongue?"

"I figured there was no sense in adding to the confusion."

"Oh," he said, "I thought maybe you were worried."

"About what?"

"Oh, I don't know." He turned and looked over the grounds, the house, shrugged and gave a little laugh. "No, you got me there, baby. Did you close your bedroom door last night because there was a draft?"

"Maybe it blew shut."

"I didn't hear it."

"Neither did I."

"It was closed when I got up," he said. He turned a little and leaned back against the door frame. "When you went down to breakfast this morning, I went in your room looking for a match and found a gal's handkerchief on the floor by the bed. I put it on the dresser and I was going to call your attention to it. But when I went back in my room that maid came in your room and I guess she took it out with her."

"She had a nerve."

"That's what I thought. But I didn't want to say anything to her and pull a boner maybe. You work fast, baby."

"Guess again, Abe. It was probably Vivian's. She woke me up at about four this morning when she found Stan wasn't in his room. Stan spent the night on the boat."

Harrigan said nothing for a minute. He kept squinting at the sunlight. Then he said absently, "Yeah. On the boat."

CHAPTER VIII

SHULTZ HAD worked for the Cantwells almost seven years. At the time of his death he was forty-five. Vivian was the only one who took his death as a personal loss and this was because when he'd first come to work for the Cantwells, she'd been a kid of twelve or thirteen and had more or less grown up under his wing.

"He used to take me to the movies sometimes," she said. "And he used to drive me to and from school and he was, well, always around. He was grumpy a lot, but he was nice, and he taught me to drive a car. Poor Oscar!"

We were lying side by side on our stomachs in the bow of Stan's cruiser with the wind in our faces. The Sound was very smooth and through the deck I could feel the muffled impulses of the engines.

"Did he ever give anyone a lift on the road?"

"I don't know. I don't think so. I remember once when I was riding with him—I was just a kid—I said, 'Oh, give that poor man a ride.' But he shook his head. He said, 'If it was my own car, I might. But I'm driving somebody else's property.' He had certain set ideas. You know, I don't believe he *did* pick up anybody on the road last night."

"It doesn't sound as if he would. What happened, then?"

"Goodness, I wish I knew! It might have been someone he thought was a friend."

"I thought Fritz said all the cars were in the garage when you asked him to look. That was about four A.M., wasn't it?"

"Yes. I asked him about that later. He said he knew Oscar wasn't in but he didn't want to say so. The help always try to cover up one another. He just thought Oscar was out on a late party."

"How long have Fritz and his wife been around?"

"Since Stan and Ivy were married. Three years."

"How about the maid?"

"Lily? About the same time. When Stan and Ivy take a trip, Lily goes along as Ivy's personal maid."

"Do you like her?"

Vivian said, "I never really thought of that."

"This fellow who's driving the boat now, doesn't he sleep on board and watch it?"

"He does as a rule, yes. But his home's in New London and he went up there yesterday to see his father. His father's an invalid. He got back this morning. That's why Stan walked over last night, to make sure he'd locked up."

Mabel Ryan's voice yelled, "Hey, sherry flips on the after deck!"

I twisted and looked around and saw her grin and beckon. She was wearing a white jersey and a pair of navy blue shorts.

Vivian said, "Coming," and we both got up. There were two steps down to the main deck and we followed the narrow passageway to the stern of the boat. Beneath a taut yellow awning were wicker easy chairs and a wicker table. Stout white forearms, spattered with freckles, were passing drinks up through a back window of the galley. Stan was taking the trays. Through the window I caught a glimpse of Harrigan's big, amiable face.

"I think," said Karen Langard, "we have a wonderful barman. Oh, Mr. Harrigan, your drinks look delicious!"

Harrigan's voice came out of the galley: "I go for brandy eggnogs myself, Miss Langard, but this time of day they're liable to take your ears off. A sherry flip gives you the lift without the sock."

Ivy, taking one of the flips, said, "I think it's terrible that Mr. Harrigan has to mix the drinks and be stuck down there preparing luncheon. Fritz could just as well have come along."

"Well, I offered to make the luncheon," Mabel said.

Ivy said, "Oh, did you? I must have been somewhere else."

"Let him," I said. "He loves it."

Mabel said, "I guess it was when we all were swimming."

"I wanted George to go in," Karen Langard said, "but he was in a vile humor this morning. Irritable. You'd think he'd been up all night. I said, 'George, a swim will do you good.' But no, he was determined to be irritable."

Roy Stockland said reasonably, "After all, Karen, you did play up to that orchestra leader."

"Jack Kingsley's a dear and I was just so overjoyed to see him again. I'm naturally affectionate, that's all."

George Hazelhurst's face looked drawn under his tan. "Just forget it, Karen, will you? Will you please forget it?"

"Well, you have no cause to get sore because I happen to meet an old friend and am polite to him."

"Listen, Karen, I am not sore. Do you understand, please? I am not sore."

"Now that that's settled," Mabel Ryan said, "let's drink. Whom shall we drink to?"

"Mr. Harrigan," said Ivy, lifting her glass. "A toast to you, Mr. Harrigan."

"This," said Harrigan, "is more than I deserve."

Stan was sitting with his elbows on his knees. The spot on his lip looked now like a fever blister. He was staring vacantly into his drink and when we all raised our glasses he remained that way.

Ivy said, "Stan."

He started. "Yes, dear?"

"We are drinking to Mr. Harrigan."

He sat up straight and lifted his glass. "Yes, sure. To Mr. Harrigan."

"A swell cook and a swell barman," I said.

"And no doubt," Roy Stockland said, "an excellent detective."

"Oh, so-so," I said.

A stiff offshore wind was blowing when we entered the mouth of the river. You could smell salt marshes. It was five o'clock and a lot of the wallop had gone out of the sun but it was still fairly high. The wind made the river choppy. Mabel Ryan was taking the cruiser in. She was handling it as unconcernedly as some people handle a car.

Harrigan said, "She's a pretty good sailor, ain't she?"

"I don't know anything about it, but I guess so. Stan's letting her take it in."

"I guess Shultzy's death kind of depressed him, huh?"

"He'd take a thing like that to heart."

"Well, you got a guy working for you seven or eight years, I guess it would."

The screened door opened and Ivy came in from the deck and made a hopeless gesture. She dropped to a green settee and wagged her head and said, "It's no use, I guess."

"What's the matter?" I said.

"Oh, George Hazelhurst. He's sore at Karen and he's going home."

"What did she do now?"

"Nothing. She said he didn't seem to be having a good time and she asked him if his stomach was upset. And he said, well, if it was, it was his own stomach. I think he just got up this morning and decided to be nasty."

I said, "He's probably still sore about that orchestra leader. Let him go home. He'll get over it."

"Sure," said Harrigan. "Absence makes the heart grow fonder."

Ivy said, "I can tell you one thing, Mr. Harrigan. I wish everyone were as kind and as considerate as you are."

"Harrigan," I said, "you've made a conquest."

Ivy looked at him and said, "It would help your friend Mr. Webb a great deal if he took a lesson or two from you."

Harrigan was amused. "Oh, Webby's all right, Mrs. Cantwell. He just gets off on the wrong foot sometimes."

Ivy turned and opened the screened door.

"Anyhow," I said, "nobody'll make me sore enough to go home."

For an instant Ivy's eyes shimmered, then she went out and the door slapped shut.

We all walked around the back of the house from the garage to the terrace. George Hazelhurst was well ahead of the rest of us, because he was going to pack his bag and go home. When we got to the terrace Pascarella and Engle were sitting there drinking beer. Both set their glasses down and stood up.

"Hello, Mr. Cantwell," Pascarella said.

Stan said, "Hello. Have you been waiting long?"

"No. Fifteen or twenty minutes is all. Look, Mr. Cantwell, did all you people here ride in that beach wagon?"

"Yes, we did—all of us, I guess, except Mr. Webb and Mr. Harrigan. We drove out to the beach club yesterday at about three to see some high diving."

Pascarella said, "Then we can leave them out. It's like this, Mr. Cantwell—and you other folks, too—they been taking fingerprints off it at headquarters and what we want to do is eliminate as many as possible. We don't like to bother you and your guests here, but it would be a great help if we could have all your fingerprints."

Ivy said, "That's ridiculous! Are we going to be constantly annoyed because our chauffeur was fool enough to give somebody a ride?"

Pascarella's gloomy expression did not change. He said, "But we won't ask you all to come to headquarters, Mrs. Cantwell. We can send a man out to get 'em. It won't take but ten minutes for all of you."

"I don't care if it would take only a minute," Ivy snapped back at him. "I'm not going to have my home overrun with a lot of policemen."

Pascarella held up his index finger. "Just one, ma'am. It takes just one man."

"Ivy's right," George Hazelhurst said mutinously. "I don't blame her a bit. I won't submit to it, either. And don't you, Stan."

Stan looked a little bewildered. "I don't know," he said.

Roy Stockland said, "Now, George, you're just upset. I can't see what harm there would be in it."

"Who's upset?" George Hazelhurst demanded. "I'm just backing up Ivy."

"Oh, come on, come on," Mabel Ryan said. "Let's all have our fingerprints taken."

Ivy's face was white. "I will not!" she cried.

"What they just want, Mrs. Cantwell," said Harrigan, "is to get these prints and check 'em with the prints they find on the beach wagon. As it is now, they won't know which is which. But if they got all our fingerprints, and the other servants' in the house too, they'll just eliminate them. Then the ones they don't eliminate, the ones that don't check with ours, they check against their own records and if nothing turns up they send them to the central bureau in Washington for a check there."

Pascarella nodded. "That's it, Mrs. Cantwell. We just take all your fingerprints here and when we've checked 'em against the ones we found on the beach wagon, we give 'em all back to you. There's no record made at headquarters. In other words, we don't keep them on file."

Ivy was tapping her foot. "I still think it's unreasonable."

"It would help us a great deal," said Pascarella.

"Oh, go ahead; say yes," Stan said. "How about you, George?"

"Come on, George," Roy Stockland said.

Hazelhurst threw up his hands. "Oh, all right, all right!" he growled, and stamped into the house.

Stan said to Pascarella, "I don't suppose you've discovered anything yet, have you?"

"Nope," said Pascarella. "And I'm not very optimistic, as they say. All we found was Shultz was over to the amusement park last night. The bartender at the Beer Barrel served him a couple of beers. He said he broke a twenty-dollar bill for him. That was about midnight, maybe a little before. The medical officer placed his death at about three A.M."

Harrigan said, "Was he alone at the Beer Barrel?"

"Yeah. He left after he changed the bill. Now we got to find where he went. Well, we probably won't. Will it be all right if the fingerprint man comes out in about an hour?"

Ivy looked at her wrist watch. "Make it seven. We dine at eight."

Pascarella and Engle picked up their hats, dipped their heads politely and walked away. In a couple of minutes there was the sound of their car going away on the driveway.

"Mr. Engle looks just like a boy," Karen Langard said. "Such a beautiful complexion! Well-built, too."

"Don't let George hear you," Mabel Ryan said.

Karen sighed. "George is certainly becoming a problem child."

"Oh, yeah?" said George Hazelhurst from an upstairs window. "Well, nuts to you! I'm going home!"

Ivy groaned, "Oh, *go!*"

We all went inside and separated, except that Harrigan and I stopped in the bar to pick up a couple of bottles of cold ale. As we reached the top of the stairs, George Hazelhurst arrived there on his way down. He carried a yellow pigskin overnight bag and a couple of tennis rackets.

"Going?" said Harrigan.

"Yes!" He was halfway down the stairs before he stopped and looked up and said, "Goodbye. Glad to 've met you both. I hope you'll forgive me." Then he rushed on down.

Harrigan said, "Forgive him for what?" as we walked into my room. "He didn't do anything to us."

We opened the two bottles of ale and sat down in chairs by the window that overlooked the terrace.

Harrigan took a long swallow, said "Aaaah!" enthusiastically, then added, "I love it but it sure gives me gas."

"Not like beer," I said.

He crossed one knee comfortably over the other. "You know, Webby. I happened to think of something. Maybe that ignition key was on a ring and there were some other keys on the ring and this guy—or gal— wanted 'em. Or maybe just one."

"Then that wouldn't make it a casual hold-up."

"That's what I was thinking."

"If you don't stop thinking," I said, "you're going to spoil my vacation."

I took a shower and shaved and by the time I had dressed it was almost six-thirty. Harrigan had gone down. When I went down, Stan was standing in the hall with his hands clenched and a flat gray color on his cheeks. Fritz was just leaving the hall. He was clasping his hands together in front of him with chest high and tight.

"Fritz see a ghost?" I said.

The look Stan gave me was glassy. I could see his chest and shoulders go down as his breath flowed out. His hands opened slowly.

He said, "I'll tell you later, Larry."

CHAPTER IX

THE MAN CAME out to get our fingerprints at a quarter past seven and Ivy had something to say about his being late. All he said was, "I'll take yours first, madam," cutting his words precisely with small sharp teeth. "Your full name?" He wrote her name down on the white card and on this card he recorded her fingerprints. Stan was next. Then Roy Stockland. Then Mabel Ryan. Then Karen Langard. Then Vivian.

Harrigan said, "Webby, maybe you and me ought to have ours, too. Just in case we touched it."

"Sure," I said.

We had ours recorded and then Fritz and his wife Emma and the maid Lily had theirs. The man was finishing up with Lily when Norman Bennett came breezing in full of bounce.

"Am I late for the cup that cheers?" he asked.

Stan said, "Do you mind having your fingerprints taken, Norman? We've all had ours. You probably know about Oscar Shultz."

"Yes, I read it in the paper. I'm awfully sorry, Stan."

"The police are looking for fingerprints on the beach wagon, and they want to eliminate ours. Do you mind?"

Norman Bennett flexed his legs, looked at everyone, smiled. "Not at all. I feel guilty already."

"Now," said the man from headquarters when he had done with Norman Bennett, "is there anyone else?"

"That's all," said Stan.

Vivian said, "But George Hazelhurst. . . ."

"Oh, yes. George Hazelhurst," Stan said. "He went home."

"Have you his address and telephone number?"

"Yes. I'll get them for you."

"Pascarella said that everyone would be here."

Karen giggled. "Oh, George got mad at me and went home. Mr. Pascarella is a very sad looking man, don't you think? And I thought Mr. Engle looked so young. He has wonderful skin, hasn't he? And a nice smile. Is he really very young?"

"Mr. Engle is twenty-eight. He is married and has two children, one aged four, the other two. He is my son-in-law. And now, Mr. Cantwell and madam, thank you for your coöperation. Thank all of you, ladies and gentlemen. Good night."

Stan escorted him to the door.

Karen Langard said brightly, "He's—he's—m-m-m—courtly. Isn't he courtly?"

Stan came back and his face let down a little and was shadowed between his eyebrows. He said, "I didn't want to tell any of you this

before he got here. I didn't want you to be upset while he was here."
He glanced at me. "There was a phone call at about a quarter to seven.
Fritz got it. Fritz answered the phone. A man on the phone told him
that Shultz's death was just a warning. Next time, he said, it would be
closer. Closer, he said. He lisped."

Roy Stockland said, "Didn't you say that someone phoned Mace
Shelby—"

"Yes. He lisped too."

Vivian groaned, "Oh, Stan!"

Ivy's face was white. She cried out, "It's because you insist on letting
Mace Shelby run the newspaper any way he feels like running it! You
own it! Why don't you do something about it? Must we all be killed
because Shelby is drunk with power?"

Stan grimaced. "Don't say that, Ivy," he pleaded. "Shelby is doing
only what he feels is right."

"I'm not blaming Shelby," she cried. "I'm blaming you! He won't
stop but you could, if you wanted, stop him."

He turned up his palms, held them out toward her. "But you know I
believe in what he's doing, Ivy. And if Shultz's death is hooked up with
it, all the more reason why we should continue."

Ivy's laugh was short, harsh, and it trembled. "Oh, yes. We should all
be killed because you and Mace Shelby have what you call a sense of
civic responsibility. Oh, yes, indeed!"

He said, "Don't worry. I'll hire some bodyguards. I'll—"

"Bodyguards! Do you think I'm going to live in this house with a
lot of roughnecks prowling around night and day? What do you think
I am?"

"Oh, Ivy, Ivy," said Vivian.

Ivy's lower lip gleamed with moisture. "Yes, and you of course will
humor him. Anything Stan wants, yes, yes, give it to him. He wants to
take me on a schooner to some Godforsaken place in the South Seas.
Just for a year, he says. Just Stan and me. Alone together. To see this
and that. To see where Stevenson is buried. To see a grave. A *grave*,
mind you! That's something, all right. Why doesn't he go? Why doesn't
he go alone?"

"Ivy!" It was Stan's voice, thick, hoarse, desperate. For a moment his
eyes looked metallic, dangerous. He said, "Control yourself, Ivy." He
meant it.

Ivy caught up her breath.

Mabel Ryan said, "If he lisps, the police ought to have a pretty easy
time finding him."

Ivy shot her a vicious glance, then said hotly to Stan, "Or take her
with you! Go ahead, take her with you! She'd love it! Go down to some
Godforsaken island and be a couple of love birds!"

Vivian stamped her foot. "Ivy, don't be an idiot!"

"Don't you talk!" Ivy cried hysterically. "I know enough about you!"

Vivian's face darkened, her nostrils flared. For a minute I thought she was going to spring on Ivy.

But Mabel Ryan's good-humored voice said, "Take it easy, Vivian. Ivy doesn't know what she's saying. If she did, I'd slap her down."

Stan started toward Ivy, his hand extended. He was calm now. "Come on, Ivy. Lie down a little while."

She drew her shoulders up and her whole body seemed to contract. "Don't touch me!" she choked. "Don't touch me!"

Stan's hand fell to his side. It hung there, tired and limp. He turned away and walked out of the living room and the back of his neck was dull red. He disappeared but a moment later there was the sound of his footfalls on the tile floor of the bar.

Ivy went upstairs.

I looked at Harrigan. He was sitting in a chair pretending he was deeply absorbed in reading a book. The book was in French. He didn't know any more about French than I did.

I was lying in a wicker long chair on the terrace fooling around with a guitar when Roy Stockland came out and sat down. For a couple of minutes he watched me trying to pick out chords.

"Do you play a guitar?" he said.

"No. I've always wanted to, though. Years and years."

"Did you ever study?"

"No. But Ivy's pretty good at this. I remember when they were casting for that play, *The Reef,* they wanted a girl who could play the guitar. Not really go to town on it, just strum it so it would make sense. Ivy learned to make a guitar make sense in one week, and she got the part. The play flopped, but she kept on monkeying around with a guitar until she became pretty good."

"I never saw her on the stage."

"Well, I only saw her in *The Reef.* It didn't call for much acting."

Stockland studied the palm of his left hand. "You don't seem to get on well with Ivy, do you?"

"We never did get on very well. I guess I just like to pick on her."

"That's often a sign of love."

"Not for long, though. She picks on Stan. That's a sign of love!"

"I believe she's extremely fond of Stan," he told me gravely. "It's simply that his attitude in this matter exasperates her. I'm very much concerned over the whole nasty business. I can understand that Stan would not want to put the damper on his editor, and at the same time I can understand Ivy's anxiety."

Karen Langard came out and said, "What do you think? Mr. Harrigan has consented to help find out who killed poor Shultzy!"

Stockland said, "You'd better check up on your alibis, Karen."

CHAPTER X

PASCARELLA STARED down gloomily at the letters which had been clipped from a newspaper and pasted on a sheet of wrapping paper to read: LAY OFF OR ELSE!

"It could mean anything," he said. "And you say the guy on the phone lisped?"

Stan nodded. "The one who phoned Mace Shelby lisped and the one who phoned here lisped."

Pascarella said, "I was practically sure it was some bum Shultz picked up. What fooled me was us finding no dough on him. Looks like robbery was just incidental."

Harrigan said, "It could still be robbery. Then the screwball that phoned Shelby could have read of the murder in the paper and figured it would be smart to phone here and say, see, I warned you, and I done this one just to warm up on."

"Yes, there's that angle too," Pascarella said unhappily. He looked at Stan. "You don't think, Mr. Cantwell, that anybody in the D.A.'s office would be whacky enough to crack back at you like this because of that stuff in your paper?"

Stan shrugged. "I never did think anyone in the D.A.'s office was responsible for either the phone calls or this thing that came by mail. But it must be somebody who's part of that political clique."

Pascarella said to Engle, "Offhand, Joe, can you think of any guy we ever collared that lisped?"

"It doesn't come to me; nope."

"I guess we'll just have to ask around. We got in touch with Shultz's brother in Rochester. He'll get here tomorrow, to take the body. We gave Shultz's room a good dusting, didn't we, Joe?"

"Yeah; you remember."

"Yeah. Maybe we ought to give it another once over."

When we reached the door to Shultz's room, it was locked.

Stan said, "Fritz has the key. I'll get it." It took him only a couple of minutes to get the key.

Pascarella and Engle went in and Harrigan leaned in the doorway. I stayed outside with Stan. They turned the lights on and though Harrigan pretty much blocked the doorway I could see them going through the dresser drawers again, through Shultz's two suitcases. Then Engle got down on his knees with a flashlight and looked under the bed. He looked under the dresser. He thrust one arm under the dresser to his armpit and when he withdrew it there was a small flat gray book in his hand.

"A bank book. Savings bank," he said. "Ha, it was you that looked under here, Al."

"I'd swear there was nothing under there when I looked," said Pascarella. "What does it say?"

"It says there's a balance of eleven hundred bucks and sixty-eight cents. He drew out five hundred on June the nineteenth. That's about five weeks ago. Wait a minute. It looks like he marked something in pencil alongside what he drew out. Here. Take a look."

Pascarella squinted at the open book and Harrigan moved into the room. Pascarella said, "It looks like Y.H., and then 6-21-37."

"That's the date," Engle said. "Two days after he drew it out of the bank. It looks like it's just a memorandum."

Stan went in and said, "What's the matter?"

"It's nothing, just this," Engle said, holding the book up. "This 6-21-37 here, and then these initials Y.H."

"That's a G," Stan said.

"It looks like a Y to me."

"Maybe. But it looks like a G to me. Some people write a capital G as a small one." He turned to Harrigan. "What do you think it is?"

Harrigan peered closely. "I think you're right. I think it's a G. The H is plain enough, all right. G.H. Probably somebody's initials. Hey, Webby, come here and look at this."

I looked at it and said I thought it was a G. "I write my G's that way," I said. "A lot of people do."

Engle said, "G.H., G.H., G.H. Guy, Gregory, Gilbert. I got a cousin named Gilbert."

"George," said Pascarella. "That's an easy one. George. When you get to the H, though, you run into trouble."

Harrigan said, "Ha, there's Harrigan."

"And Hazelhurst," I said. "There's George Hazelhurst."

Pascarella squinted at me. "Wasn't he the lad made all that stink about his fingerprints we wanted?"

"Yes," I said. "He was just irritable, though. He was that way all day. Upset."

"Upset all day, was he? He was upset all day, huh?"

Stan said to Pascarella, "He's pretty crazy about Miss Langard and if she so much as looks at another man, he blows up. I don't think you need worry about George Hazelhurst."

"Oh, I'm not worrying," Pascarella said. "I'm just asking questions." He put his hands on his hips, stared at the floor. "After we left here this morning, who locked up here?"

Stan said, "Fritz, I guess."

Pascarella sent Engle to fetch Fritz and when Fritz came through the doorway, owl-eyed, Pascarella said, "Did you lock up here after I left this morning?"

"Yes, sir."

"How long after?"

"Gee, I don't know. I guess maybe half an hour."

Pascarella's expression was not hopeful when he said, "You didn't chuck a bank book under that dresser, did you?"

Fritz put his head on one side and looked as if Pascarella had asked him something in a strange tongue. Then he looked at Stan, for help.

Stan said, "Mr. Pascarella looked under the dresser when he was here this morning and says there was nothing there. A little while ago Mr. Engle looked and found Oscar's savings bank book. Mr. Pascarella wants to know if you put it there."

"Oh, no," said Fritz, in dead earnest. "Oh, no, sir. What would I be doing with Oscar's bank book?"

"Okay, okay," said Pascarella. "When you locked up, what did you do with the key?"

Fritz pulled a ring of keys out of his pocket. "I keep 'em all here. This one, this is it."

"Oh, so you had a key to this room?"

Fritz nodded. "Yes, sir. When Oscar was away, maybe weeks at a time, driving Mr. and Mrs. Cantwell, I cleaned the room here. I had to get in."

"Was there any other key?"

"No, sir."

"Didn't Shultz have a key?"

"Oh, yes. Sure. Yes, sir. I thought you meant—"

"And where did he keep his key?" Pascarella asked.

"Gee, I don't know, I guess like me, on his keyring."

"Did you ever see his keyring?"

"Well, it wasn't a ring like this. It was a leather thing, with the keys on hooks inside."

Harrigan said, "Automobile keys too?"

"Yes, sir. I seen it hanging from the ignition switch in the beach wagon, so I guess so."

"There you are, Pascarella," Harrigan said.

"There I are—am—what?"

"The ignition key was missing from the beach wagon because whoever knocked off Shultzy wanted one of the keys."

Pascarella said, "The key to this room?"

"Your guess is as good as mine. What do you think, Mr. Cantwell?"

Stan looked bewildered. "I don't know," he said. "If Oscar was killed as a warning to me, why should the murderer want a key to his room?"

"Offhand, I'd say to get something incriminating and destroy it." Harrigan said.

"After the crime had been committed?" Stan asked.

"Sure. Maybe the crime was committed because Shultzy had something on somebody. Shultzy missed his calling when he didn't make the cops. He liked to snoop. Did he know about that warning you got?"

"Yes. And he knew about the phone call Mace Shelby got."

Fritz said, "Excuse me, please. Yes, Oscar said at breakfast the other day, he said he was going to look around a lot of tough joints and listen for anybody that lisped and he said he was going to ask questions."

"Did you see any strangers around here at all today?"

"No, sir. I wasn't here all day, though. From two to four, I wasn't. I drove my wife to the dentist."

Harrigan said, "And we were all out on the boat."

"Then there was nobody around here?"

"Oh, yes, sir. Lily was here," Fritz said. "Miss Maguire, the maid, she was here."

"And after I left, this room was open for about half an hour, you say?"

"Yes, sir. About. When I came out to lock up, Miss Langard said wasn't it all terrible and I said, yes, it certainly was."

"What else did she say?"

"She said Oscar must have been a very neat man, the way his room looked."

"You mean she was in here?"

"Yes, sir."

CHAPTER XI

GOING AROUND the corner of the house in the moonlight I heard a piano being played with a kind of delayed rhythm that sounded very good. I could barely hear it but as I crossed the terrace and entered the bar, it was plainer, nearer, and I guessed it was in the living room. Mabel Ryan was behind the bar banking at chuck-a-luck and Roy Stockland and Norman Bennett were in front of it betting.

"Is that Vivian at the piano?" I asked.

"Karen," Mabel Ryan said. "Vivian's upstairs. I guess trying to get Ivy to face the fact that after all, my dear, you are the hostess. How is the law doing?"

"They'll all be along any minute."

Stockland said, "Perhaps Ivy'd better stay upstairs then. If she sees a lot of detectives roaming about the place—well, you know Ivy. You may remember that Pascarella promised her that only one would come out tonight."

Mabel said, "Well, Stan phoned them to come out when we got up from the dinner table."

"I thought Harrigan was going to take charge," Norman Bennett said.

I said, "He is. He told Stan to notify the cops. A couple of cops get to kicking ideas around and every once in a while they pick up one that winks back at them. The more cops the better. That's nice piano playing."

"Karen probably feels sentimental," Mabel said. "I think she really likes George Hazelhurst. This might be an opportune time for you to try a little missionary work."

I went into the living room and leaned on the piano, watching Karen's fingers on the keys.

"Nice going," I said.

By way of reply she put words to the melody: "The very thought of you . . . *do-do do do-do do.*" She looked past my shoulder, nodded, smiled to someone.

Then Pascarella put his elbows on the piano alongside mine and watched her fingers also. Engle came up on the other side and she gave him a very large smile. When she had finished the song, Harrigan said:

"Can you play 'Time On My Hands'?"

"If you will sing it, Mr. Harrigan," she said.

"Listen," said Pascarella. "We don't want to hang around here all night. Look, Miss Langard, I just want to ask you a few questions. Do you mind just keeping your fingers still a minute?"

Norman Bennett and Roy Stockland came in with Mabel Ryan between them. Stan looked tired.

Pascarella said, "Miss Langard, I hear that after we left this morning, Fritz went out the garage to Shultz's room and you were standing there."

"Oh, yes. Yes, I was. Did you lose something?"

Pascarella shook his head dourly. "No, miss, I didn't lose anything. I was just wondering what you were doing in Shultz's room."

Karen laughed, "Oh, that. Well, I wanted George to play tennis with me. George Hazelhurst, you know. But he wouldn't play. So I went outside and I saw Mabel going in Shultz's room and I went in and asked her if she would play."

"Mabel?" said Pascarella.

"Me," said Mabel Ryan.

"Oh," said Pascarella, turning to look at her. "Well, what were you doing in there? I look under the dresser this morning and there's nothing there. I look under it tonight and find Shultz's bank book. Did you put it there?"

Mabel chuckled. "Listen to the man!"

"Well, what were you doing in there?"

"Gosh, I don't know. The door was open and I just went in and looked around. Maybe it was morbid curiosity. You see, I've known

Oscar ever since he came to work for the Cantwells. How do I know why I went in? Is there a law against it?"

"Did Miss Langard ask you to play tennis?"

"I don't remember."

"Why, Mabel, I did too," Karen cried in an injured tone.

"All right, but I don't remember, Karen."

Pascarella said to Karen, "Well, if you asked her to play tennis, what did she say?"

"Now wait," Karen said. "Let me think. Oh, now I know what happened. I meant to ask her but just as I got there Lily the maid came out and told Mabel she was wanted on the phone. No, you're right, Mabel I didn't ask you. I'm sorry. I only meant to."

Pascarella sighed. He said, "And then you stayed in Shultz's room?"

"Just a couple of minutes. It's interesting to see the kind of pictures people have on their walls. That's what I was doing when Fritz came in. Pictures of baseball players and fighters mostly, and I thought that one of Jack Dempsey was very good—very aggressive. Did you notice it?"

Pascarella looked moodily at Engle and said, "Come on, Joe. We'll go over and pay a call on George Hazelhurst."

"Give him my love," Karen said. "Tell him he's just being a silly little boy."

When Pascarella and Engle had gone out Roy Stockland said to Karen in a chiding voice, "If you really loved him, Karen, you'd phone him and tell him that the police are coming."

She looked scared. "Do you think I ought to?"

Stockland changed his manner and said seriously, "All joking aside, I think one of us ought at least to phone him and tell him to hold his temper."

"I wouldn't," Harrigan said. "You can all just take it easy. I don't think anybody is going to hang Shultz's death on Hazelhurst."

Stockland said, "I don't think so, either. But if George loses his temper. they might lose theirs and he might get hurt."

"Yes," said Karen. "I think I'd better phone him. We'll all feel better. I know I will." And she hurried off to the library.

Fritz came into the room then saying, "Mr. Cantwell, the four guards are here. They're in the kitchen."

"Will you want to see them, Mr. Harrigan?" Stan asked.

"Yeah, we both can talk things over with them," and he followed Stan and Fritz toward the kitchen.

When Karen came back her face looked puzzled. "I couldn't get George on the wire. The desk clerk at the hotel says he didn't come in today or tonight at all, any time. He says earlier this evening that man from the police, the fingerprint man, was by looking for George but he wasn't in. I had the operator ring and ring the apartment. I'm worried about him."

"He probably went some place else," I said.

"But where, where?"

"At any rate," Mabel Ryan said, "he's certainly looking for a nice big eight-ball to get behind."

CHAPTER XII

THE WIND FROM the hills that had blown late that afternoon was gone at eleven. The Sound was calm, the moonlight lay on the water like a sheet of luminous silk. The road ran along the edge of the water and the glare of Harrigan's headlights poured over the edge and brought out the rocks in sharp relief. Harrigan was taking his time.

He said, "You know, Webby, a night like this brings back a guy's youth. It kind of gets in under your ribs."

"It's sure a swell night, all right."

"Clara was nuts about moonlight on the water. Her favorite song was 'When I Dream About the Moonlight on the Wabash.' You think this is the right road?"

"I think so. We should come to a monument and turn left."

The road curved away from the water, and in a few minutes we came to the monument and turned left. We drove along between two rows of trees whose tops arched over. Then we came out and across a wide flat plain we saw the water again and in a minute we came to the club.

We went up to the veranda and Harrigan stopped a waiter and said "Go in and ask the orchestra leader to come out here first chance he gets."

"What's the name, please?"

"Oh, tell him George Hazelhurst would like to see him."

The music stopped in about five minutes and Kingsley appeared several minutes after that. Harrigan, leaning against the veranda rail, beckoned to him.

He said, "I didn't think you'd remember my name, Mr. Kingsley, but I figured you'd remember Hazelhurst's."

Kingsley studied him curiously.

Harrigan said, "We were all in Mrs. Cantwell's party last night. Miss Langard brought you over to the table. This here is Larry Webb. I'm Harrigan."

"I have a hard time remembering people. In my business, you say hello, goodbye, to so many."

"Sure. That's why I told the waiter to say it was Hazelhurst. I figured you'd know that one."

"Yes, I know him."

"That's what I thought. I saw you and him having an argument out by the parking lot. I thought it was funny when Miss Langard introduced you all around that you and Hazelhurst didn't say anything. You know, like hello, well, glad to see you again, George; glad to see you, Jack."

"Maybe I'm slow to catch on, Mr. Harrigan. What's this all about?"

I said, "Harrigan's a retired cop. He's doing this for a friend."

"Well, what do you want to know?" Kingsley asked.

"Suppose I asked you what you and Hazelhurst were arguing about last night?"

"He asked me to do him a favor. He just got sore because I wouldn't say yes. I told him I'd think it over."

"I guess you don't want to say what it was about, do you?"

Kingsley shrugged. "I'd rather not. It's a personal matter. When a fellow's down, you don't like to kick him in the face, do you?"

"What do you mean by down?"

"Well, I guess Hazelhurst's trying hard to make a living."

Harrigan said, "He must have been a pretty good friend of yours."

"No, there wasn't anything like that."

"Oh," said Harrigan, jingling change in his pocket. "I get it. Business."

Kingsley looked at his watch. "You'll have to pardon me. I'm a working man."

"Just one more question, Mr. Kingsley. If I had, say, a couple of thousand bucks and I wanted to do business with Hazelhurst, what would you say?"

Kingsley smiled. "I don't think you'd do business with anyone, Mr. Harrigan, without being pretty sure about your money."

"You learned from experience, huh?"

"Good night," Kingsley said. He turned and strode inside.

I said, "Well, it was a nice ride over, Abe."

"Sure. And we found out that Hazelhurst once did business with this fellow and probably took him over."

We walked back to Harrigan's roadster. A couple of miles up the road he braked hard and swung in alongside a low white clapboard building that said Sailors' Rest—Beer and Ale On Draught. We stood at the bar and ordered ale. The barman laid down a newspaper he was reading and picked up two glasses. Harrigan turned the newspaper around and looked at it.

"Well," he said, "I see Shultzy made the front page."

The barman said, "Tough, wasn't it?"

"Name me something tougher."

The barman shoved our ale across the bar. "Yeah, sure was. Here I'm talking to him last night and today I read he's dead. I been depressed ever since."

Harrigan said, "What time was it you saw him last night?"

"It must have been between eleven and twelve. He only stopped for a beer. He was on his way to the amusemnt park."

"Was he alone?"

"Yeah. I asked him to hang around and play a little pinochle but he said he had a date over at the amusement park."

"Some girl, I guess, huh?"

The barman nodded. "I guess so."

"Know the girl?"

"Nope. But I think she worked over there some place. I know he said he had this date for twelve-thirty. I says, 'Tough hours for a girl.' And he says, 'Plenty. And her boss pays her fifteen bucks a week and she probably handles that much in an hour.' Oscar always hated to see people take advantage of other people."

"I guess it was a cashier he had a date with," Harrigan said. "How do we get to that amusement park?"

We parked the car in a big cinder lot· back of the roller coaster and a kid with a flashlight stuck half a ticket under the windshield wiper and gave the other half to Harrigan. We took an alley between the roller coaster and a dime museum to the main stem. Everything was crowded. I smelled peanuts roasting and bought two bags and gave one to Harrigan.

He said, "Let's take a ride on the merry-go-round."

We went in and got on and stood next to each other on the edge, so we could try for the brass ring. Harrigan was ahead of me and got a ring each time. He looked over his shoulder and said, "There's Pascarella," and pointed. Pascarella was standing inside the door. He tossed up a finger and we both waved back at him. When we dropped off Pascarella said:

"I thought I recognized you guys."

"Do you live around here?" Harrigan asked.

"I came out to talk to that bartender at the Beer Barrel again. Sometimes a guy will forget something and if you ask him again he'll remember it."

"Did he?"

"Oh, no. I didn't think he would but you can never tell."

Harrigan said, "I found out Shultzy had a twelve-thirty date here from a guy that runs a beer stube on the shore road. It sounds like it was some dame that's a cashier."

"Maybe we could ask around."

"Yeah. We'll start from here. You go that way and I'll go this and we'll come back here."

"I'll wait here," I said. "I'll wait over there by the shooting gallery."

They walked off in opposite directions and I went over to the shooting gallery and picked up a rifle and took a row of ducks down. A metal disc was swinging back and forth and I tried that and got four out of six.

Harrigan came back and said, "Okay, Webby. Let's find Pascarella."

"Did you find her?"

"Yeah."

We walked a couple of blocks and saw Pascarella coming out of a soft-drink place.

"She works in the Blue Point Grill," Harrigan said. "Come on."

She was sitting on a high stool back of a cash register. She was plump, about thirty-five, and wore nose glasses.

Harrigan said, "Miss Polinski, this is Detective Pascarella. Tell him what you told me."

She took a breath and after a scared look at each one of us she said to Pascarella, "Well, Mr. Shultz called by here for me after I finished up and we drove into town and had a hamburger at Jimmy's Diner, that's on Little Street, and then he drove me home. I live on Jackson Street, number two-twenty Jackson Street. Well, that's all we did. I said good night and Mr. Shultz went home."

"When did he leave you?" Pascarella asked.

"It must have been about half-past two. I was tired and so was he and he said he was going right home."

"Did he say a thing about being frightened about anything?"

"No. Only last night he asked me if I knew anybody that lisped and I said no, I didn't."

"What else did he say?"

She took another breath. "Well, it was just something about where he worked. He said if things didn't change soon he was going to find another job. He said he was sick and tired."

"Of what?"

"Well, he didn't say. I asked him but all he said was, 'It burns me up when a woman like you has to work like you do, and no complaints, and then some other dames get everything from a cold start and are never satisfied.' That's all he'd say."

We went outside and Pascarella said, "Well, he left her place at two-thirty and it would take him, say, fifteen minutes to get from Jackson Street to the Cantwell place. Seven or eight miles. Only he never got there. He must have given some guy a lift."

"I hear Hazelhurst wasn't at the hotel," Harrigan said.

"No. Instead of going to his hotel he stopped at the Athletic Club for a shave and then had dinner there. I showed him the bank book with the G.H. in it. He said it was five hundred bucks Shultz gave him to invest in some bonds. I said we didn't find any receipt for the dough or any bonds and he said, well, he gave him a receipt and he named the bonds. So I figure Shultz must have had a safe-deposit box in one of the banks. We'll find out. His safe-deposit box key must have been on the ring with others that were taken. What we're going to find is that Shultz simply gave a bum a lift and the bum slugged him. But if I don't examine all the angles, the inspector'll stand on his head."

Harrigan and I got in the car and drove off.

"Webby," he said, "much as it's probably going to pain some people, we got to find out something."

"I know. That shot we heard."

"Yeah. We got to find out for sure whether it was inside the house or out."

I said, "Did you ever stop to wonder if possibly Shultz fired it?"

"I asked him. You remember when me and him were standing in front of the garage and you come over? I'd just asked him. He said no. He said he thought it was probably over in the woods."

"Did you ever stop to think that maybe somebody took a pot-shot at Shultz then?"

"It don't add up, Webby. The guy that killed Shultzy killed him because he wanted something connected with one of the keys on that keyring. I don't think he would have killed Shultzy if Shultzy would have given in. If that's right, then no one would have taken a pot-shot at him. But I ain't worried as much about that shot as I am about something else."

I didn't ask him what else it was he was worried about. But in a minute he said:

"I wish Stan Cantwell had some way of proving he slept on his boat."

We pulled into the garage at midnight and walked down the driveway toward the house. Four floodlights had been rigged up, one at each corner of the house, and the grounds were drenched with the white glare. Two cars, one of them a limousine, were parked in the driveway. We went into the house and through the living room to the bar.

Triangular sandwiches, thin slices of chicken on thin slices of white bread, were banked on a silver tray on a table. Mabel Ryan came in with a cone-shaped silver coffee pot.

Ivy was there in an apricot-colored ensemble: pajamas and robe to match. Anger and unrest, and perhaps some crying too, had scared her eyes and the shadows beneath them were deep purple. The arrival of the guards and the setting up of the floodlights hadn't helped her any.

"No, thank you," she said when Karen passed the sandwiches.

Karen said, "A bite to eat will do you good, Ivy. They say that if you eat something before going to bed the digestive organs go to work, they draw the blood from the brain and so you sleep better. Just a bite, Ivy?"

Ivy's smile was polite. "No, thank you, Karen."

I leaned against the bar and asked Harrigan to look in the icebox and see if there was any milk there. He set out a pint and then dumped it into a tall glass.

I said, "Harrigan, you look very natural behind the bar. I think you're a better bartender than you are a detective."

Karen Langard said, "I do so think Mr. Harrigan is a good detective. I do. It's a woman's intuition."

"I never was crazy about being a cop, Miss Langard," Harrigan said. "When I was a kid I wanted to go out West and be a cowboy but my old man was against it. My old man was a stevedore. He said, 'Abe, get a job you can be proud of and get one that'll give you a pension in your old age. Don't be like me,' he says. 'Work today; laid off tomorrow. Get on the cops, Abe,' he says. And then I met Clara Boylan and her old man was a cop and I began to think, 'Pop, you're right. Some job with a pension.' You should've seen me in my first uniform."

One of the guards strolled by outside. At his left hip was a holstered gun, the butt jutting forward.

Ivy's exasperated voice muttered, "We're like a lot of goldfish!"

"I got two around the house," Harrigan said, "and two down around the gate. With these floodlights on all night, nobody can get near the house without being seen."

Roy Stockland said, "Have you searched the house completely—that is since the guards arrived—to find out if anyone is *inside* the house? It's a large house and there are a number of places where someone might hide."

"No guy in his right mind," said Harrigan, "would try to do anything inside the house, when you got all those floodlights outside, and men on patrol."

Stockland said, "The inference all along has been that the person who sent Stan that warning and made those telephone calls, one to Mace Shelby and the other to the house here, is not exactly in his right mind."

Ivy started, then lay back in the chair and put her hand to her breast. Stan, in pajamas and robe, had come silently into the doorway. He was smoking a pipe.

"You frightened me," Ivy said breathlessly.

"I'm sorry," Stan said. "I thought I smelled coffee cooking and it smelled good."

"Sure," said Mabel Ryan, jumping up. "Have some."

Norman Bennett winked. "Stan's Girl Friday."

"What was that, Norman?" Stan said.

Vivian said, "Oh, Norman's talking to himself. Don't pay any attention to him."

"Yeah?" said Norman Bennett. "Well, I guess I might just as well be talking to myself. I was all right to knock around with until a certain party turned up from New York. I was all right, I was, wasn't I? Yeah. Barman, fill 'er up."

"No!" cried Vivian, her cheeks flushing. "When he gets tight, he heckles people. He heckled George Hazelhurst last night and he knows George can't stand being kidded that way."

"See?" said Norman Bennett. "I'm in the dog-house now. I was all right, I was, until this certain party came up from New York, but now I'm just a heel."

I finished my drink of milk and said all around, "If you'll excuse me, I think I'll go to bed."

"Why don't you go home?" Norman Bennett said.

Karen Langard said, "Oh, he's been referring to Larry Webb all along!"

"Yeah," said Norman Bennett. "Larry the Webb. He must certainly have what it takes. Nice girls leave handkerchiefs in his room."

I was on my way across the bar and I stopped and picked up an empty beer bottle and turned around.

Harrigan said, "Keep it clean, Webby."

Stan ripped the bottle out of my hand. "Take it easy, Larry," he said. "He's a little tight. You know how people are when they get tight."

"Sure," Norman Bennett laughed, "he knows how people are when they get tight. He knows everything. He knows how to get a nice girl's handkerchief——"

"Stan, let me go!" I yelled.

"Sure, let him go," Norman Bennett said.

Stan shouted, "Shut up!" He was strong and he held my arms behind my back and tried to pull me out of the bar.

Norman Bennett came striding over and I knew he was going to hit me but I knew that Stan didn't think so. I tried to roll with the blow as much as I could. Both Stan and I went down.

Mabel Ryan said in a stormy voice, "You dirty coward!" I'd never seen a girl look so outraged in all my life. She swung and he wasn't looking for it and it took him under the chin and he went down hard.

Stan jumped up and I sat on the floor and rubbed my jaw. I wasn't worried about Norman Bennett because he was out cold. He was sprawled on his back, his arms and legs limp, one pants cuff twisted up to his knee.

Vivian said, "Are you all right, Larry?" She was bending over me, her dark red hair hanging like a wave across one eyebrow and down her cheek.

"I'm all right."

"Are you sure he didn't hurt you?"

"I'm all right."

"He hit you when you couldn't defend yourself——"

"Vivian, don't be maudlin!" Ivy broke in. "He's been practically asking for a punch in the jaw ever since he arrived! I know him! Norman's right! Why doesn't he go home?"

Roy Stockland was standing with his hands pressed flat against his thighs, his chin on his chest, his eyes frowning at the floor. His lips were grim; the angles of his lean face made sharp shadows. Karen Langard was looking out the door and patting her hair and making believe she hadn't heard a word. Stan was opening and closing his lips, trying to say something, the right thing. Vivian was glaring at Ivy and for a minute I thought she might walk over and slap her face. Mabel Ryan was examining the knuckles of the hand with which she'd hit Norman Bennett.

Harrigan's shoes slapped the tile floor leisurely but definitely as he came from behind the bar bearing a pitcher of water.

"Aqua," he said, unloading the water on Norman Bennett's face, "Aqua pura. I learned that from one of my waiters."

On my way up to my room I met Vivian on the staircase. She put her hand on my arm and said, "Don't go home, Larry. Don't take Ivy seriously."

"I'm not going home," I said. "I'm going to bed."

"But tomorrow, I mean; don't go home tomorrow. Don't get mad. Don't fly off the handle."

"What should I have done, just said 'boo' to Bennett?"

"He didn't know what he was saying, Larry?"

"He knew what he was saying. The maid found your handkerchief in my room. She must have told him."

She swallowed. "Was that what he meant?"

"What did you think he meant?" I asked.

"I really don't know. I thought he was just trying to be funny. I didn't know I'd lost it."

"Harrigan found it and put it on my dresser and while he was in his own room getting dressed the maid came in mine to straighten up. She must have found it."

"I'll bet Mr. Harrigan has a swell opinion of me."

"No, I told him how it happened."

"You won't go home, Larry, will you?"

"I don't think Harrigan will let anybody go home."

She tipped her head to one side and squinted at me. "What do you mean by that?"

"He wants to settle something. He wants to settle whether that shot we heard was inside the house or outside the house."

"But no one's said any more about it, and no one was hurt."

"He still wants to settle it. Are there any guns around in the house anywhere?"

She shook her head. "No. Stan's always hated guns. He won't have any in the house."

"Do you know if Shultz had one?"

"I don't know. I don't think so. You frighten me, Larry."

"Well, don't be frightened. Just lock your door when you go to bed, and leave the key in the lock. Have you got a bolt on your door?"

"No. Ivy's the only one who has a bolt."

"What's she afraid of?"

She dropped her eyes. "I don't think she's afraid of anything, really. It's a just a whim."

"When did she get this whim?"

"Oh, a month or so ago. Before all this trouble began."

"How long have Ivy and Stan been sleeping in different bedrooms?"

"Is there anything wrong about a husband and wife sleeping in separate rooms?"

"That isn't what I asked you."

She said, "You've certainly got it in for Ivy, haven't you?"

"I never saw a woman yet who didn't answer one question with another. I haven't noticed you throwing love and kisses her way."

"I've tried, Larry. I've tried desperately hard to be nice to her." She shivered. "But she's cold. She's cruel. She's selfish. The way she talks to Stan, regardless of who's around!"

I took her elbow and we went the rest of the way up the staircase together. At the top I said, "Now, Vivian, how long haven't they been sleeping in the same room?"

"Oh, I don't know, a month or six weeks."

"From about the time she put the bolt on the door?"

"About a month or six weeks," she said.

"Why did she put it on?"

"I told you, I don't know, a whim! How do I know?"

"Okay, Vivian."

I went to my room and undressed and by the time I was putting my pajamas on Harrigan came into his room, came through the bathroom into my room. He showed me a keyring on which there were four keys.

"Me and Stockland carried Bennett to bed," he said. "But I tucked him in. I pulled his pants off and held them upside down so everything would fall out. I put everything back but his keys."

"What have you got on him?"

"Nothing. But two will get you ten if he hasn't been playing around with the maid Lily."

"I thought he was making a pretty big play for Vivian."

"All right, the other was just on the side and maybe the maid's nuts about him. She probably gave him that handkerchief she found in your room. She must have. Okay. He has a grudge against George Hazelhurst and the second time Pascarella dusts Shultzy's room he finds Shultzy's bankbook, with the G.H. in it alongside a five-hundred-buck withdrawal. The bankbook was planted there, it must have been, between Pascarella's first visit and his second, and if it was, it was planted there to chuck suspicion on Hazelhurst. If the maid is ga-ga over Norman Bennett, why couldn't he have given her the book to plant in Shultzy's room?"

"I suppose you're going to stand there and tell me that Bennett was walking along the road between two and four in the morning and Shultzy stopped to pick him up. Ha!"

"All I know was that Bennett didn't sleep here and that he wears the same size shoe, size eight, that Shultzy wore. And when they found Shultzy dead, he was minus his shoes. I'm going to take a ride over and take a look at the place Bennett sleeps. You coming?"

"Guess again. I'm going to bed."

"If I find anything, I'll wake you up."

"It'd better be awfully good."

CHAPTER XIII

When I went downstairs at half-past nine Sunday morning Harrigan was eating breakfast in the dining room.

"You the only one up?" I said.

"Nope. Miss Mabel Ryan talked Mr. Cantwell into going for a swim. Haven't seen anybody around."

"Good morning, Mr. Webb," Fritz said.

I said, "Hello, Fritz. Fruit, any kind of cereal, toast and coffee."

Fritz went away and I asked Harrigan, "Anything doing at Bennett's?"

"A little." He took a small green cardboard box from his pocket, threw it in front of my plate. "Half full."

It was half full of .22 caliber cartridges.

"All right; where's the gun?"

He shook his head. "No gun."

"Listen," I said. "You know Bennett wasn't around here when we heard that shot. He and Stan came home from the boat in the beach wagon afterward."

He said, "I found these cartridges in Bennett's room but there was no gun there. That's all I know. Maybe he lent the gun to somebody."

"Where is Bennett?"

"Still sleeping it off. I had a phone call from Pascarella this morning. They got a flock of cops on the river road. Also a troop of boys scouts. They're looking for a pair of shoes."

We finished breakfast at about the same time and Harrigan said to Fritz, "When Mr. Bennett gets up, tell him I want him to stay here." He said to me, "A little walk would do us good. Come on."

The morning sun was hot and it wasn't tempered by a breeze. Walking down the driveway it was cooler but when we came out in the open, at the gate, it was hot again.

We turned left and strolled up the road. Going that way, the road led to the city; the other way, to the beach. In about ten minutes we saw a couple of cops and a couple of boy scouts batting around in the brush alongside the road. They were all along the way, in pairs or groups.

The gravel pit was a mile from the gate and by the time we got there we were perspiring but perspiration didn't seem to bother Harrigan. Beneath a large shade tree Pascarella and Engle were sitting on the running board of their car.

Harrigan said, "Hello. Do you expect to find anything?"

"Nope," said Pascarella. "It wasn't my idea. The inspector thought it was a good idea, and here we are. Here," he said, taking a brown envelope from his pocket. "Them fingerprint records. They're all there. Give 'em back to the people, will you? Hazelhurst's is there too."

"Sure," Harrigan said.

"By the way, Shultz's brother got in this morning, to claim the body. He'll probably run out to see Mr. Cantwell."

Harrigan looked up and down the road. "Well, let's get back, Webby."

"We'll give you a lift," Pascarella said.

When we reached the gate Harrigan said, "This is okay. Thanks a lot."

We walked up the driveway among the big evergreens and found Norman Bennett lying in a wicker long chair on the terrace. He grinned.

"I want to apologize, Webb," he said. "I lost my head."

"You'd have lost it if Stan hadn't grabbed the bottle out of my hand."

"I hope you'll accept my apology."

"Maybe I'm not the one you ought to apologize to."

"I didn't mention any names, you know."

"I did, though."

He sat up. "What do you mean?"

"I told Vivian it was her handkerchief the maid found in my room and gave to you."

His hands slapped down on the arms of the chair and his shoulders hunched. "Why, you dirty rat!"

"Get out of my way, Harrigan," I said.

Harrigan said, "Shut up." He straight-armed me out of the way and said to Bennett, "Stay put. I want to ask you something."

Bennett couldn't have got up if he'd wanted to, for Harrigan sat down on the foot of the long chair and jammed a hand down on his knee. "Easy, pal," he said. He used his other hand to draw keys and the box of cartridges from his pocket. He tossed the keys and they hit Bennett's belt buckle. "There's your keys," he said. "I took 'em out of your pocket last night and went over and took a look at your room. I found these cartridges there."

"You've got a sweet nerve taking my keys."

"I didn't want to wake you up. Where's the gun you shoot these things out of?"

"I lent it to Shultz."

"When?"

"A week ago."

"What kind of gun was it?"

"You've got the cartridges there. What kind do you think it was?"

"I know it was a twenty-two. Was it a rifle, a revolver or an automatic?"

"A rifle, a rifle."

"What did Shultz want a rifle for?"

"He said there were some rabbits raiding his vegetable garden and he wanted to get 'em."

"Did you give him some cartridges too?"

"He helped himself to some."

Harrigan said, "Did he give you the rifle back?"

"No. You didn't find it in my place, did you?"

"Nobody found a rifle in Shultzy's place, either. What do you think about that?"

"Maybe he hid it somewhere," Bennett said irritably. "Stan was dead against guns."

"What time was it when you left here night before last?"

"I don't know, exactly," Bennett growled. "When I got home to my cabin the one next door was lit, so I went over and sat a while with the cashier from the club, Charley Myers. It was about three when I turned in, I guess. I suppose you think I killed Shultz?"

"What makes you think I think you killed Shultz?"

"What makes me think! You've asked me to establish an alibi!"

"That's for your own benefit, Mr. Bennett. What I'm trying to find out is what happened to the gun you lent Schultz?"

"What does it matter? Was Shultz killed with a gun? No!"

"What I don't want," said Harrigan patiently, "I don't want anybody else to be killed with a gun. Especially a twenty-two." He stood up. "Okay, that's all." He pointed a finger at me. "Now you keep your trap shut, Webby."

Bennett got up, shot me a contemptuous look and walked off across the lawn.

Fritz came out with a mop and Harrigan said, "Where is everybody."

"The beach," Fritz said. "They all went to the beach."

Harrigan said, "Open Shultz's room for Mr. Webb, will you? Webby, take another look around. Look good."

"Ask Fritz," I said. "Fritz, did you ever see Shultz with a rifle?"

"Once," Fritz said. "You see, when I came to work for Cantwell I had a little rifle, just a little, single shot, an old one, and Mr. Cantwell wouldn't let me keep it. He had no use for guns around the place. Oscar knew that too, but—well, he kept this vegetable garden, and something was always ruining it, so he borrowed a gun and he figured maybe to use it when Mr. Cantwell wasn't around."

Harrigan said, "Did you think that's what that shot was the other afternoon?"

"Yes—yes, sir, only I didn't want to say, I didn't want to get Oscar in Dutch."

Harrigan made a weary gesture. "Okay, Webby, take a good look for it, will you?"

I followed Fritz out back and he opened the door to Shultz's room and I felt like a fool looking around after everyone else had looked around. I looked in the bedroom and in the bathroom. Then I sat down on the bed and smoked a cigarette. I got up and turned back the mattress but there was nothing there and there was nothing beneath the box spring. I looked all over the garage and climbed a ladder to a storage space above. I spent fifteen minutes poking in trunks and boxes and didn't find anything. On my way back to the head of the ladder I saw an old canvas golf bag with a hood on it hanging on a nail. It was covered with dust. The hood had a zipper and the zipper was held shut by a small lock. Shultz's initials were on the bag. I took it down with me and broke the lock with a screw-driver and found eight golf clubs and a .22 caliber rifle.

Harrigan wasn't downstairs anywhere. I finally found him in the upstairs hall.

"Where'd you locate it?" he said.

"In Shultzy's golf bag."

We went into my room and Harrigan took the rifle and stood by a window with it. It was a single-shot rifle and he broke it at the breech and smelled it. Then he squinted through it.

He said, "Now, you'd ha' thought Shultzy would ha' told me he fired it."

"He probably thought you'd make some crack in front of Stan."

Harrigan closed the rifle and stood it against the wall.

"I been looking around in the rooms," he said. "Come on; I want to show you something."

I followed him out of my room and into a bedroom that overlooked the driveway on the west side of the house. He went directly to the windows. There were two windows and both were open. He pointed to the one in which there was one of those ready made screens you can make wide or narrow, according to the size of the window. He touched his finger-tip to the black tin strip down the center.

"This strip was bent and then straightened again. When it was straightened, some of the black enamel chipped off. This is the screen Shultzy was holding in his hand when you and me stood with him there in front of the garage, late the first afternoon."

"I remember now," I said. "He was straightening it."

"Yeah. It must have fell out of this window and he must have picked it up and was straightening it. Only by just falling on good soft grass, this middle strip couldn't get bent the way it was. It was knocked out. Hard. A fist or an elbow or a shoulder or something chucked at it."

I looked around. "Whose room is this?"

"It's the one George Hazelhurst was using." He pointed down at the lawn below. "You remember I called your attention to a gouge down there I said somebody must have made with a niblick? There, you can see where it's been stamped back in place."

"You're going to tell me it was made by the screen when it fell and I'm going to tell you the screen's not heavy enough."

"Oh, no, I'm not. I'm going to tell you that it'd have to be something heavier and harder and that by the way the turf was lifted, something that was spinning when it hit. A revolver, for instance."

"Or a hammer."

"Or a revolver."

"Or an axe."

"Or a revolver."

"Well," I said, "it looks as if we're going to have George Hazelhurst with us again."

He pointed at the window. "From here, what do you see?"

"I see a big oak tree, part of the driveway, part of the garage, part of a stone wall with woods beyond."

"If Shultzy'd been standing in front of the part of the garage you see, which is the part where he lived, he would have seen this window. If the screen was knocked out he would have seen it. And he would have seen who knocked it out. And he would have seen a revolver fly out."

"You keep harping on the revolver. Go get Hazelhurst."

"Okay, I keep harping on the revolver for two reasons. One is because I heard a shot and the other is because I seen and you seen that gouge in the lawn when it was fresh and while it ain't likely a guy would have an axe or a hammer up here, he might have a gun, and something hard that was spinning made that gouge in the lawn."

"All right. Why was the screen knocked out and why did the gun fly out?"

"An argument. A tussle."

"Between who?"

"Between Hazelhurst and somebody else. I don't know. Maybe his girl Karen Langard. Or Mrs. Cantwell. Or Stockland. Or Miss Mabel Ryan. They were all up here. How do I know? Am I a magician?"

"Go phone him."

"Yeah. Maybe on Sundays he ain't antisocial."

CHAPTER XIV

DRIVING ALONG Broad Street, the sun was directly overhead. The shops and department stores were closed and the sidewalks were almost deserted. Harrigan stopped long enough to ask a cop how to get to the Tremont Hotel. It turned out that we were only half a dozen blocks from it.

It was a seven-storied red brick building with white window ledges. We didn't stop at the desk. We went right into the elevator and Harrigan said, "Mr. Hazelhurst's apartment." And when the operator had run us to the fifth floor, "Which one, boy?"

It was 510. Harrigan flopped a brass knocker up and down and in a minute Hazelhurst opened the door.

"Sunday callers," said Harrigan. "Do you mind?"

"Well—it's a surprise, anyhow."

Harrigan said, "I tried my best to get you to come out."

"Nothing doing," Hazelhurst said, throwing up his hands. "I've had enough of that madhouse."

We went in and Harrigan nodded to a couple of traveling bags; they were open, partly packed. He said placidly, "Going somewhere?"

"Yes. I'm driving up to the Cape for a couple of days. Maybe a week."

"Now look," Harrigan said. "A murder's been committed and—"

"Can I help it? What am I supposed to do, wear mourning because Shultz was killed? I tell you I'm going to the Cape."

"No," said Harrigan, shaking his head. "No, Mr. Hazelhurst."

Hazelhurst's lip curled. "I submitted to having my fingerprints taken when I didn't have to, but I'll be damned if I'm going to let you talk me into anything else! I'm going to the Cape."

"Shultz gave you five hundred bucks. You say it was to buy bonds with."

"Yes, and he got the bonds and I gave him a recipt for five hundred dollars."

"They ain't been found. If we find them, okay. But I want you to come out to the house."

Hazelhurst slammed a shirt into his bag. "Nothing doing! What, go out to that madhouse? Nothing doing!"

"Of course," said Harrigan, shrugging, "if you don't want to go of your own free will, I'll just have to notify the cops."

"Go ahead. They can't hold me for anything."

"Don't you believe it. They can pick you up and toss you in the can. They don't have to book you for twenty-four hours."

Hazelhurst thrust splayed fingers against his chest. "You'd do *that* to me?" he demanded.

"I'd do it to Webby here too, if he argued with me."

Hazelhurst dropped his hands to his sides. He stared at the floor, his teeth champing at his lower lip.

Harrigan said, "Bring along things for overnight."

Hazelhurst shot him a dark, rebellious look. Without saying anything, he emptied one bag and then repacked it and banged it shut. His manner changed. He was almost laconic when he said:

"All right, let's go."

"We can all go in my car," Harrigan said.

"If you don't mind," Hazelhurst said tersely, "I'd rather go in my own."

"Okay. You lead the way. We'll follow."

Hazelhurst got in his car and booted it off so hard that the motor whined. He tore through the streets but Harrigan had no trouble keeping up with him. When he pulled up in the driveway in front of the garage Fritz came out and said luncheon was being served in the pavilion.

Harrigan said, "We'll go upstairs a minute," and Hazelhurst told Fritz he'd carry his own bag up. He barged in through the back door and was up in his room by the time we reached it. His set expression indicated that while he had come out here he was not going to break down and be agreeable.

"Look," said Harrigan, "I asked you about a shot I heard Friday afternoon—"

"And I told you I didn't hear it. Maybe you did hear a shot. I told you I was taking a shower about that time."

"Did you ever have a .22 caliber pistol or revolver?"

"No."

Any kind of revolver or pistol?"

"No."

Harrigan tapped the window screen. "This screen got knocked out of this window sometime Friday afternoon. Do you know when?"

"No. I don't remember it at all. I couldn't tell you if it was in the window or out of it. All I know it that Friday about noon Shultz came up and put it in. He said the regular one was being repaired. I know he put it in but I don't remember it being out later."

"When you took the shower, how long were you in the bathroom?"

"As long as it takes a man to bathe and shave. Fifteen or twenty minutes. How do I know?"

"When you came back in this room, did it look the same as when you left it to go to the bathroom?"

Hazelhurst sat down and held his jaw in his hands. He stared bleakly at the floor. "I don't see how you can expect a man to remember every little detail when he's not thinking of details."

"Was anything different in here? Was the furniture changed? Was the rug scuffed up? Did you smell powder smoke?"

"No, no, I don't remember—Wait a minute," he said irritably. "When I came back in, yes, when I came back in I pulled a shade down halfway to keep the sun out. It was all the way up. Not the shade at the window with the half screen in it; the other one, this one. The other one was halfway down, the way most shades are. I pulled this one down to match it. I don't think it was up when I first came in from playing tennis. If it had been, the sun would have struck me in the face when I came in the door, the way it did when I came from the bathroom." He stood up. "Wait a minute. I left the door open when I went to the bathroom. I remember propping a chair against it. When I came back, the door was closed."

"Where was the chair?"

He pointed. "Where it is now. That green enameled chair."

"Have you touched it since then?"

"No."

Harrigan bent down, grasped the chair by two of its legs and said, "Okay, Mr. Hazelhurst. Come on, Webby." He carried the chair to his room, set it down very carefully. He said, "Baby, Hazelhurst's room is the kernel of the nut we got to crack."

"Was he telling the truth?"

"You can answer that as well as me. It will all come out in the wash."

I said, "Know what I think? I think all this stuff about Hazelhurst getting sore enough at Karen to go home was all a build-up. He just wanted to get out of this house?"

"Sure. That's why I wanted him back here."

"What are you going to do with the chair?"

"Take it to police headquarters and have it processed for fingerprints. Want to go along?"

"I feel like food," I said. "Goodbye."

That gave him an idea and he hesitated and then looked anxiously in the direction of the pavilion. But finally he sighed, shook his head. "No. I better go now." He looked as if he were making a great sacrifice. He went out.

A guard was coming along the flagstone walk when I came out on the terrace. Behind him was a small, bony man in a pearl-gray suit and a Panama hat.

The guard said, "We stopped this man at the gate. He wants to see Mr. Cantwell. His name's Shultz, he says."

"Oscar's brother?"

The little man nodded. "Yes, sir. I'm Leopold. I come down from Rochester and the police said Mr. Cantwell wants to see me."

"I'm sure he does," I said. "I'm awfully sorry about your brother, Mr. Shultz."

"Yes, sir. It was a shock. We ain't writ each other in years. It was a shock."

I said, "If you'll wait here, I'll get Mr. Cantwell."

"Okay, yes, sir."

I walked back to the pavilion, where everybody was eating. They were still in bathing suits.

"Stan," I said. "Shultz's brother is here. The terrace."

"Oh, yes," Stan said, getting up.

Karen Langard rose too. "Oh, we must all go and express our sympathy. All the way from Albany. The poor man."

"Rochester," Mabel Ryan said. She stood up and tossed her hair back off her forehead.

Roy Stockland got up and slipped into a white terry-cloth beach robe, and Vivian, saying "There's plenty to eat, Larry," went off with him.

I sat down and picked up a stalk of celery.

Stan had paused at the edge of the pavilion.

"Coming, Ivy?"

"No. Give him my condolences."

"I think you ought to come, Ivy."

"I'm not though."

"But, really, Ivy—"

She stopped him with a look. Her voice thickened when she cried, "I tell you I'm not going!"

He came back to the table. "Ivy, I want you to come with me and merely express your sympathy to Oscar's brother." His voice was clear, grave. "It's the decent thing to do."

Her eyes shimmered, her lips tightened against her teeth. "I am not," she said precisely, "going. Is that clear?"

He inhaled. His fingers closed into his palms. Then suddenly he flicked the edge of the table with his knuckles and strode swiftly away.

I helped myself to potato salad, baked ham, baked beans, green olives, and lettuce from a wooden mixing bowl.

"This is a nice place to eat," I said. "Cool. Especially on a day like this. George Hazelhurst's back."

"Marvelous," she said. "I suppose love conquered all."

"Listen, why be a mugg? Go out and say you're sorry to Shultzy's brother."

"I will not be maudlin."

"Listen, Ivy. One thing that gives me a pain is a small-town girl that grows up to the tony."

She gave a brittle little laugh. "I never really fell for you, did I, Mrs. Webb? And you never really got over it."

"Ivy, no kidding, you can certainly put it on. I remember that the first time I introduced you to Stan you told me afterward, 'Nice but dumb.' I agreed with you. Then you found out that he had dough."

Her hands slapped the table. "You contemptible louse!"

"When I phoned Stan on long distance before coming out Friday, were you listening in on an extension?"

Her face was twisted with contempt as she said, "As if I'd care what you said!"

"Somebody was. Pass the pepper, will you?"

She picked up a glass shaker and threw it at me. I caught it but some of the pepper had sprayed out and for a minute or two I sat sneezing. The more I sneezed the madder I got.

"What do you want to do, blind me?" I choked.

"I'd like to do something to you," she said in a cold, dry voice. "I thoroughly hate and detest you."

"Sure. I was all right to introduce you to guys in the show business but after Stan married you—or you married him—I was just scum. And you know why, sweetheart."

"You hated to see me marry Stan didn't you?"

"You know why, sweetheart. Your show flopped, you were broke, you were a second-rate actress, and there, all at once, was a big, simple, nice guy with loads of jack, and he was nuts about you. If I'm wrong, check it. Today you can't bear to have him touch you. There's a bolt on your bedroom door—"

Her voice grated. "You vile—you vile—"

She stood up. Her eyes looked murderous. I was watching her hand because it was near a waffle iron and I didn't want her to throw it at me. But a step on the pavilion stairs drew her attention. Stan was there with Leopold Shultz.

Stan said, "Ivy, this is Oscar's—"

She turned on her heel and strode to the back of the pavilion and vaulted over the rail. I saw her cutting down toward the house.

Stan called, "Ivy!" and ran after her.

Leopold Shultz remained where Stan had left him, on the top step of the pavilion stairs. He had his hat in his hand. With his other hand he was fingering his chin.

I said, "Think nothing of it, Mr. Shultz. Mrs. Cantwell's not herself today."

"It's funny, all right."

"What?"

"Her. She looks much like a girl I used to know in Rochester. Maybe ten, fifteen years ago. Over us in a flat they lived. The old man drove a brewery wagon and was always drunk. The old lady was terrible, fighting all the time. And they had this girl that all the time would pick on my daughter and once near to scratched her eyes out. I don't know whatever happened to them after the landlord put them out. I think they moved out to the country somewhere." He shrugged out a small, reminiscent laugh. "Funny how you think you see people you knew. I remember this girl, her name was Marie Traynor."

"I'm always seeing people who remind me of other people," I said.

"Sure. Sure. Well, I got to be going. I got a taxi waiting. It runs up. In Rochester, I'm a waiter. I don't get back, some other feller my job gets. Goodbye."

He walked down the stone steps through the rock garden, reached the driveway, followed the driveway past the house. I heard a car drive off.

In a few minutes Vivian came back to the pavilion and sat down beside me. "Oscar's brother was wondering if there were any insurance papers," she said.

"They'll probably find out he had a safe-deposit box in one of the banks, when they look tomorrow. They'll be there, probably. They also had better find some bonds Hazelhurst said he bought for Shultzy and a receipt for five hundred bucks. Otherwise Hazelhurst is going to be a very unhappy young man."

Vivian said, "Karen is trying to make him come out of his room. He won't come. He said he was brought out here against his will and he's just going to stay in his room. Do you think he had anything to do with the murder of Oscar?"

"There's only one thing I'm absolutely sure of, Vivian: I didn't kill Oscar. Anybody else might have killed him. Harrigan might have killed him. I'll ask Harrigan if he killed him."

"Be serious, Larry."

"All right, Stan could have killed him. He says he spent the night on the boat. Who knows if he did? The boat was only about a half a mile from the gravel pit where they found Shultz dead in the beach wagon."

She held her breath for a minute, then let it out slowly. "That's what I've been afraid of all along. Fritz said that at about eleven o'clock Oscar Shultz came into the house and said he wanted to see Stan, he wanted to tell him something. But Fritz told Oscar that Stan had gone to bed."

I nodded. "I heard them talking. Fritz told Shultz he ought to mind his own business—in a nice way, you understand. Shultz had quite a grouch on it. It was probably his feet. He was complaining about his new shoes hurting him."

I put the fork down suddenly and looked in the direction of the garage.

Vivian said, "What is it?"

"Shultz's shoes," I said.

CHAPTER XV

HARRIGAN SET THE green enameled chair down in the center of Hazel-hurst's bedroom. He looked at it as though it were a rare antique about which he knew a great deal. He waited patiently until everybody was in the room.

He said, "The way I remember it, when me and Webby arrived here Friday afternoon, Fritz was out back wiping this chair off. He'd just taken it out of a crate. After you took it out of the crate, what did you do with it then?"

"I brought it up here to this room. It was a chair Mr. Cantwell bought for this room."

"Was this door open or shut?"

"Shut. I knew Mr. Hazelhurst was playing tennis, so I opened the door and brought it in."

"Okay," Harrigan walked around the chair without taking his eyes off it. "Did you see this chair brought in, Mrs. Cantwell?"

Ivy shrugged. "No. If I had, I might have had it taken right out. It doesn't go in this room at all."

"Did you come in this room at all Friday afternoon?"

"No."

"And you didn't see the chair when it was downstairs?"

"Goodness, no!"

"That's funny," said Harrigan blandly. "Because outside of my own, there's three sets of fingerprints on this chair. Mine's down on the legs, where I picked it up. The others are up here on the top of the back, where you naturally pick up a chair to move it. There's Fritz's here: he brought it up. And there's Mr. Hazelhurst's: this is his room, and there's yours, Mrs. Cantwell."

"Are you trying to insinuate that I was in this bedroom with George Hazelhurst?" Ivy demanded.

"All I asked was, was you in here? I know you touched this chair, but maybe you touched it while it was downstairs."

She snapped, "Maybe I did touch it. I didn't notice if it was this chair. I happened to walk past this room and the door was open and there was a draft. The draft was blowing things around in the room. There was a chair propped against the door and I pushed it out of the way, picked up some stationery from the floor and put it back on that writing desk. But if you mean to stand there and insinuate that I was here alone with George Hazelhurst—" She turned to Stan. "Are you going to let this man say a thing like that?"

"All he asked you was a question, Ivy," Stan said levelly. "You've answered it; now let it go at that."

Harrigan said, "Mrs. Cantwell, when you come to this door and it was open, were you blinded by the sunlight coming through that left-hand window?"

"I don't remember."

"Mr. Hazelhurst says that when he came back from the bathroom and opened the door here, the sun blinded him because that left-hand shade was all the way up. Do you remember if this little screen here was in or out of the window?"

Exasperation was making her lips twitch. "No, I don't remember that. I told you what I did and I probably wouldn't have recalled doing that if you hadn't practically insulted me."

"Lady, I'm the last guy in the world to insult a lady. Can't I ask some questions? There's something happened in this room. At least, I believe there did. Sometime during the afternoon that little screen there was knocked out of the window. It didn't fall, understand. It was knocked out. Because," he said, walking over to it and pointing, "this piece of tin down the middle was bent. I seen Shultzy fixing it out in front of the garage about ten minutes after I heard that shot."

Stan said, "I thought it was settled that the shot you people heard was fired from a rifle Shultz had borrowed from Norman Bennett to shoot a rabbit that was raiding his vegetable garden."

"It makes sense, all right," Harrigan said, "but it don't settle anything. You just suppose the shot was fired from Shultzy's gun that he borrowed."

"Do you mean someone else fired that rifle?"

Harrigan shook his head. "No. I mean maybe that shot was fired from another gun. Whether it was fired inside the house or outside, is open to argument. Mrs. Cantwell says she thought it was a blow-out or a back-fire. Mr. Hazelhurst says he didn't hear it at all. Miss Langard says she didn't hear it. Well, he was in one bathroom at about that time and she was in the other, and they say they were taking showers. So that'd make sense why they didn't hear it. Mr. Stockland said it sounded like a twenty-two all right but he thinks it was in the woods. Fritz and his wife think it was Shultzy taking a crack at a rabbit. Miss Ryan here says she was taking a snooze at the time and didn't hear it. And Webby, never the one to commit himself, says it could have been inside or out, from the sound of it. The maid didn't hear it but she says she was running a vacuum cleaner in her room about that time."

Hazelhurst laughed. "And we're all out of step but you, Mr. Harrigan. You're the only one who believes it was in the house."

"To me, yes, it seemed like it was indoors somewhere."

Stockland said, "That ought to be easy to settle, Mr. Harrigan. If the shot was fired indoors, the bullet would have lodged somewhere. And if someone removed the bullet, the mark would still be there, wouldn't it?"

"It could have gone through a window," Harrigan said.

"With screens in all the windows? Wouldn't you see a bullet-hole in the screen?"

"Not if the screen was knocked out first," Harrigan said.

Stockland nodded thoughtfully. "Yes, you're right there. You're right there, all right."

Karen Langard's face brightened under the impact of an idea. "Oh, look, we can have a hunt. You know, like an egg-hunt; only make this for the bullet! Don't you think that's a marvelous idea? We'll each chip in a dollar and the person who finds the bullet—"

Harrigan turned toward the window. I heard a car's wheels moving on the driveway, then a faint conclusive crunch as they stopped outside. Harrigan leaned on the windowsill.

"Hello, Pascarella," he said.

Pascarella's voice droned up: "Well, I guess you can pick up your tools and go home, Harrigan."

The man handcuffed to Engle was about five feet tall and looked as if he might have weighed about a hundred pounds. His forehead was domed and beneath it his features were drawn tightly into a knot. There was a crooked bony insolence about his jaw. His ears stuck out from his head. His eyes were big, sharp alert, and shone too much. He looked cocky.

Pascarella stood with one foot on the ground, the other on the edge of the terrace, and was leaning with his elbow on his knee. He said, "We get a tip from a newsboy that a guy that lisps is in the railroad station waiting for a train and we go over there and collar this here guy. He's got a ticket to Boston. So just on a hunch we pick him up and make him take us where he lives. He lives in a rooming house across from the Empress Theater. His brother-in-law owns it. His brother-in-law's the boss in the fifth election district. In this here tomato's room we find two blackjacks, a pair of brass knuckles— You got the list wrote down, Engle. Read it."

Engle read from a small notebook, "One dagger, one clasp knife with four-inch blade, one cleaver, one pair brass knuckles, two blackjacks, one .25 caliber automatic pistol, one .38 caliber revolver, one twelve-gauge sawed-off shotgun, one 30-30 rifle, twelve boxes of ammunition, assorted." He closed the book and slipped it into his pocket. "That seems to be all."

"We ask him what's the idea of the arsenal and he says it's a museum he's getting together," Pascarella said. "He's either the world's biggest liar or the worst screwball I ever run across."

The man said, "Yeah, thath wha' you thay, thath wha' you thay."

"Oh . . . he lisps!" cried Karen Langard.

Pascarella said, "On a calendar in his room we found Mr. Shelby's phone number wrote down. This is the guy, all right. Imagine. We spend four hours with a flock of boy scouts looking for a pair of shoes and then get a hot tip and find this guy with a ticket to Boston. I called Shelby up and made this guy say something to him on the phone. Shelby's pretty sure it's the voice that called him and threatened him that day."

Stan said, "Who's his brother-in-law?"

"Vince Pagliano. This guy's name is Rudnicki. I brought him out here so that servant of yours could hear him talk. You know, the guy who got the phone message here."

"Yes; Fritz."

"I'll get him," Vivian said, going inside.

Harrigan sat down. "What's he claim?" he asked Pascarella.

"Oh, he says he sent that warning all right, and he says yeah, he phoned Shelby. But he says he didn't knock off Shultz. That's what he says now. Tomorrow he'll be claiming self-defense. He's been yelling for a lawyer already."

"You'll thee, you'll thee! Wait'll I thee Vinth!"

Harrigan said, "You didn't find any shoes, huh?"

"Ha," said Pascarella.

"How about his fingerprints?"

"I don't expect to find 'em on the beach wagon, if that's what you mean. This guy ain't that dumb. But I found a ticket for a ride on the Ferris wheel at the amusement park in his pocket. I called them up and give 'em the serial number on it, and found it was sold the night Shultz was killed. So little palsy-walsy here was out there at the amusement park. Give us time, and we'll put all the pieces together."

Vivian came back with Fritz and Pascarella said to him, "Can you remember exactly what that guy that phoned you said?"

Fritz dipped his head. "I think so, yes, sir. He said, 'Shultz was first. Next time it'll be closer. Say that to Cantwell.' "

"Say that, Rudnicki," Pascarella said.

Rudnicki yelped, "No!" He began to fight the handcuff and yell about his brother-in-law. Engle, taken by surprise, almost fell down. Pascarella stepped back and took a fistfull of Rudnicki's shirt, at the chest. He held up his other hand, the palm flat, ready to strike. Rudnicki stopped fighting.

"Now say it," Pascarella said.

Quivering, Rudnicki said, "Thulzth wuth firtht. Nexth thime it'll be clother. Thay that t' Canthwell."

"Sound like it?" Pascarella asked Fritz.

Fritz looked worried. "Well, it was like that, tongue-tied like that, but it was on the phone and on the phone I guess it'd sound different."

"We ought to get him on a phone," Engle said.

Stan said, "There's a dial phone in my room, separate from the house line. Or there's one in my wife's room. You can just dial the house number from either one."

"Okay. You go up with Engle and this guy and dial it, will you? Then you, Joe, make Rudnicki say that again."

They went upstairs and in a couple of minutes the phone in the main hall rang. Fritz picked it up and listened. Then he said to Pascarella, "On the phone, now, it sounds more like it. Except this time that feller sounds so mad."

"Okay. He would." He took the phone from Fritz. "Engle? Okay. Come on down."

Engle just about carried Rudnicki down the stairs. Rudnicki was tussling and making angry animal sounds.

"What's he saying?" Pascarella said.

"Same baloney. Says he made the first call to Shelby, but not the one here."

Pascarella said, "He'd be a dope to admit it, sure. Okay, Engle; take honeybunch out to the car." He said to Stan, "You'll hear more about this tomorrow. I'll give you a ring after I see the district attorney."

He went out.

"Well," said Ivy, "now we can get rid of those ridiculous guards."

"Yes, I guess I can tell them," Stan said.

Harrigan said, "I wouldn't."

"Don't you believe Pascarella has the right man?"

"He might, but I don't think so."

"But you didn't say anything when he was here."

"No, I didn't. Pascarella has a bird in the hand and all I got is one in the bush."

Vivian said, "Larry thought of something too."

Harrigan looked at me. "Webby? You don't mean to tell me Webby actually's going to commit himself to something."

I said, "The boy scouts didn't find the shoes Shultz wore because the shoes are outside in his room. When he left here Friday night at eleven I heard him complain to Fritz about his new shoes hurting his feet. When we all looked in there Saturday morning, there were four pairs of shoes there. Two black pairs, a brown pair, and a pair of white ones with brown tips. They were the new ones. Rubber soles and rubber heels, with the design of an eagle cut in the sole. The police have a plaster cast of the shoe print they found leading away from the beach wagon. You can check it up easily enough. The guy that killed Shultz put his shoes on and walked back here and with the keys he stole let himself in Shultz's room to get whatever it was Shultz wouldn't give him. When he got it, he put his own shoes on and left Shultz's in the room."

Harrigan's small eyes were bright, alive. "What would you say he got out of Shultzy's room?"

"I don't know. But you said that that gouge outside in the lawn under Hazelhurst's window could have been made by a gun spinning as it hit. Maybe Shultz picked the gun up and refused to give it back to who-ever owned it. Maybe whoever owned it took a shot at Shultz while he was standing out by the garage and then accidently dropped it."

Harrigan said, "That part don't sound reasonable."

"All right, but it helps fill out."

Hazelhurst said, "It gets madder and madder. I don't know why I came out here again."

"Why did you leave in the first place?" I said. "And what did you take away in your bag besides your clothes?"

I thought he was going to come at me, but if that was on his mind he changed it after taking two steps. His mouth looked very grim.

Ivy headed out of the room, saying, "I know what I'm going to do. There doesn't seem to be any way of getting rid of some people here, but there's nothing preventing me from going to a hotel until this cheap comedy is over."

Her heels drummed up the staircase.

George Hazelhurst said, "I'm going too!"

"I'd like to have you around here," Harrigan said patiently, "but of course I got no authority to keep you here. On the other hand, all I have to do is phone Pascarella and ask him to pick you up."

"Baby, please," said Karen Langard, patting Hazelhurst's arm.

He waved a hand aimlessly. "I'm the goat here, that's what I am. I get asked all the questions. Is that fair? Has he asked Stan any? Stan spent the night on the boat. I'm not saying he did anything. I'm just offering an example. The night Shultz was killed, Stan was on the boat, he says. Just an example."

Stan's shoulders moved in an almost imperceptible shrug. He said, "Anyone's at liberty to ask me any questions he wants to. But I couldn't have got into Oscar Shultz's shoes. I wear a size ten shoe."

Harrigan said, "If Rudnicki wasn't kidding when he said he didn't make that second phone call to the house here, then somebody else must have made it. It come in about an hour after you left, Mr. Hazelhurst. It's easy to talk tongue-tied, especially on the phone."

"All right," Hazelhurst shot back at him. "If it's easy to talk tongue-tied on the phone, then the call could have been made right in this house. Didn't Pascarella make Rudnicki call the regular house phone here from the dial phone in Stan's room? Put that in your pipe and smoke it!"

"I was in my room at the time," Stan said.

"All right, all right!" Hazelhurst hammered on. "There's a dial phone in Ivy's room, isn't there?"

Fritz came in and said, "Mr. Harrigan, could I see you outside a minute?" Harrigan went out with him.

Mabel Ryan said, "I think I'll get dressed," and the others said they thought they would too. But Stan came back and we went outside together.

CHAPTER XVI

HARRIGAN TOOK a pocket-knife and unhurriedly began digging into the window ledge. The window ledge was beneath a window of Shultz's room that faced the rear of the house. It took Harrigan a couple of minutes to pry the lead slug out.

Fritz was saying, "I remembered what Miss Langard said about maybe we should all look around . . ."

Harrigan rolled the slug in the palm of his hand. He said, "It ain't the type was in that box of cartridges Bennett had. This here is a twenty-two, all right, but it's a hollow point."

Harrigan squinted at the ready-made screen in the window of Hazelhurst's room. It was about twenty feet higher than Shultz's window, about a hundred feet away from it. You could have stood in Hazelhurst's room and, firing from an angle, you could have hit the part of the garage where Shultz's room was located.

Stan said, "Maybe it was fired from the woods over there. Maybe this fellow Rudnicki was prowling around in the woods."

Harrigan said, "Coming from the woods, it would've plowed in this ledge from left to right. Here, it plowed in from right to left—from the direction of the house."

"I don't see," Stan said, "how anyone could have been foolish enough to take a shot at Shultz from the house."

"I don't say anyone took a shot at Shultz. But maybe Shultz thought they did."

"But don't you suppose he'd have told me?"

"Webby says he heard him tell Fritz Friday night that he wanted to go upstairs and tell you something. Fritz told him you went to bed. That right, Fritz?"

"Yes, sir," Fritz said.

Harrigan said, "The way it looks, it looks like there was a tussle for a gun in Hazelhurst's room. The screen got knocked out and Shultz, back here, heard it fall. He started over to pick it up when the shot went off and the gun flew out the window. He seen whoever it was in the window. He picked up the gun and wouldn't give it back. Somebody wanted it back bad enough to clout Shultz over the head and kill him in order to get it. The phone call to the house here was a fake. It was made to chuck suspicion on whoever made the first one to Shelby and sent that threatening message to you, Mr. Cantwell. If Hazelhurst didn't make it when he left here, then it was made right here in the house, from either the dial phone in your room or the one in Mrs. Cantwell's."

He flipped the lead slug, caught it deftly in his hand, and strolled into the house. I walked along with Stan. He looked bewildered, anxious.

"Do you think George Hazelhurst did it?" he asked. "He ran away, he went home, and then when you and Harrigan went to his hotel, he was getting ready to leave for the Cape. Of course, he was probably sore at Karen."

I said, "Not sore enough to put on an act like that, though. He left here for one of two reasons. Either to take something away in his bag or because he was afraid that Jack Kingsley, the orchestra leader at the beach club, might be invited here."

"What about Kingsley?"

"They know each other. Harrigan saw them out back of the club Friday night."

There was nobody downstairs when we went in. Only Harrigan. Stan said, "Everybody's probably getting dressed. I think I will too." He went upstairs. I sat down at a table with Harrigan and in a couple of minutes Fritz brought in some food and set it down before him.

Harrigan ate deliberately, neither faster nor slower than he usually ate. But he didn't say anything. Every now and then he glanced blankly at me, or tipped his head so that he could look into the living room. When he had finished, he laid his big freckled hands affectionately on his stomach.

"That's better now. Nothing like food." He lit a cigarette and said, "Well, Webby, what's on your mind?"

"I don't know," I said.

He said, "Well, I know what's on mine."

I didn't ask him what it was because I was much more interested in what was on my own. The thing that was on my own, the main thing, had been keeping me unpleasant company since Leopold Shultz left the pavilion, got back into the taxi that had brought him, and went away.

"Maybe," Harrigan said dreamily, "we ought to call the whole thing off and go home."

"Your tootsies getting cold?"

He squinted into space. "What's on my mind, Webby, is that maybe somebody's going to get burned and our host ain't going to like it. Do you think Mrs. Cantwell will go to a hotel?"

"If you let her, sure."

"You think I should put up a kick?"

"If you let her go, then you'll have to let Hazelhurst go. Her finger-prints and Hazelhurst's fingerprints were on that green enameled chair."

"Well, she said she closed the door on account of a draft."

I said, "Do you remember any wind blowing Friday afternoon? Don't you remember putting up your windows and mine, and leaving the doors of the connecting bath open? And was there any draft at all?"

He shook his head. "Nope. I remember now." He leaned back and said, "When I took that chair in to have it processed for fingerprints, while they were doing it, I phoned that orchestra leader Kingsley and talked turkey to him. He said what happened. It was down in Miami in 1934. Hazelhurst did some finagling on a real estate deal, and it cost this guy Kingsley several grand. He said it got in the courts and Hazelhurst got a suspended sentence and he couldn't operate in Florida any more. He says, though, maybe Hazelhurst learned a lesson and is okay now."

I sat thinking over what was on my mind for a while, and then I said, "Ask Ivy if she ever knew Shultz in Rochester."

"You ask her."

"No; you. If I so much as open my trap, she'll jump down it."

"Why's she got it in for you, Webby?"

"She knows I know she married Stan for his dough."

"Well, a lot of women do that."

"Sure. It's none of my business. It's his dough, not mine, and if he gets fun out of it, swell. But the minute she married him she cut Webb off the invitation list. She couldn't stand having me around when he was around."

Harrigan rubbed out his cigarette. "He sure don't seem to be getting much fun for his money."

Mabel Ryan came down with Roy Stockland, who wore a horizontally striped silk pull-over and a pair of tan linen slacks. He said, "Stan says you found a bullet."

"Yeah, a spent one," Harrigan said. He showed it in the palm of his hand.

Mabel Ryan came over and picked it up. "What is it, a twenty-two?"

"Yup," said Harrigan.

Mabel said, "Look, Roy."

Stockland held it between thumb and forefinger, turned it round and round.

Karen Langard came into the bar with George Hazelhurst.

Stockland said, "Ever see what happens to these after they hit?"

"What is it?" said Karen, taking it from him. "Oh, a bullet! Why, of course! George, look, they found the bullet!"

Hazelhurst had gone over to lean against the bar. "I believe you," he said. "Now find the gun and everything will be dandy. Then maybe I can go home."

I saw Fritz hurrying through the living room on his way from the kitchen.

Stockland sat down and stretched out his legs. "Where did you find it?"

"Fritz found it," Harrigan said. "In the window ledge out there in the garage. Shultz's window."

He leaned a little to one side, peering into the living room. Fritz was on his way through with a suitcase, a hat box, a handbag. Behind him were Ivy, Vivian, Stan. Vivian and Stan were on either side of Ivy; they were talking to her, making urgent gestures. Ivy's face was cold, determined.

"Mrs. Cantwell. . . ." Harrigan went toward the living room. "Just a minute, Mrs. Cantwell. Now look—"

"I shall be at the Hotel Soundview—"

"Ivy," Vivian urged, "please be reasonable, Ivy."

"You, Fritz," Harrigan said. "Just stay there."

Fritz started to put down the bags.

Ivy said curtly, "Fritz, take those bags to the garage." She looked around the room. "Stan refuses to drive me to the hotel. Who will drive me?"

Harrigan said, "Fritz, just wait there a minute. Mrs. Cantwell listen to me—"

"Possibly you all think I'm acting like an idiot. Perhaps I am. But I simply will not stand another minute of—"

"If I let you go," Harrigan said, "I'll have to let George Hazelhurst go."

"Let him, let him! That's a good idea. George, will you drive me to the hotel?"

Karen Langard was holding George Hazelhurst's arm. "Oh, don't make him, Ivy. Now that he's here, don't make him."

"I'll drive you, Ivy," George Hazelhurst said.

Harrigan made a half turn. "Take my advice and stay here."

"All right," Ivy said coldly. "How about you, Roy? Will you drive me?"

Roy Stockland said, "If you insist, Ivy. But I'd rather stay here. Look at the trouble George got in by leaving."

"I don't care who drives me," Ivy said, "but I'm leaving."

Vivian said, "All right, then, if you want to be an idiot, I'll drive you, but I think it's rotten manners."

"You tend to your own manners, Vivian, and I'll tend to mine. Fritz can drive me. Fritz, take those bags out and put them in one of the cars." She crossed the room.

Harrigan said, "I'll let you go if—"

"*You* will let me go!" she cried derisively. "You have nothing to say about it. Remember, you have no authority over anyone here."

He moved with a heavy swiftness and took the bags out of Fritz's hands. "I'll say okay, Mrs. Cantwell, if you let me look in your bags."

"Mr. Harrigan," Ivy said in a voice that quivered with fury, "give Fritz those bags. Give them to him, I tell you!"

Harrigan dropped the bags. They thumped. Fritz started toward them. Harrigan said, "Let 'em alone." He said to Ivy, "Did you ever know Oscar Shultz in Rochester?"

Her eyes sprang wide open and her right hand smacked, flat-palmed, against her mouth.

George Hazelhurst said, "Don't let him bull-doze you, Ivy. Come right back at him."

Ivy staggered. I didn't think she was going to faint but she did. Stan caught her before she hit the floor. He said:

"I think you've carried this far enough, Mr. Harrigan."

"Just about, Mr. Cantwell," Harrigan said. "It's up to you whether you want me to open the bags."

"If it will make you feel better, open them." Stan had missed completely the inference in Harrigan's tone. He turned and carried Ivy out of the living room.

Harrigan remained rooted, indecisive.

Karen Langard said, "Of course, my opinion may mean nothing at all, but I don't see, I don't believe, it sounds ridiculous—I mean, Ivy killing Oscar Shultz. I know you read about women having affairs with their chauffeurs, but after all is said and done, Shultz was definitely not the type Ivy would fall for and besides—"

"Karen, be a nice, quiet little girl," George Hazelhurst said. "For once, Karen; just for once."

Harrigan said, "Well—" he dropped to one knee—"you start something you gotta finish it."

He unstrapped the suitcase, opened it so that its two sections lay flat on the floor. From among pieces of lingerie he drew a green metal strongbox about a foot long. But instead of a keyhole it was fitted with a small combination lock that worked like those on regular safes. The lid was bent, twisted, as if it had been forced open. It popped open when Harrigan pried at it with his fingers.

Lying on top of some papers was a revolver with a short barrel. Harrigan picked it up at the very end of the barrel, laid it on the turned back metal lid. He shuffled the papers. He spoke like a man thinking aloud: "Life insurance, accident insurance, receipt from G. Hazelhurst for five hundred bucks." He sighed. He put the papers and the revolver back into the metal box, slapped shut the lid. He thrust the box under his arm, got up, rubbed the back of his neck.

Vivian groaned from somewhere deep inside her, "Oh, oh!" Her fingers were pressed round her throat, a tragic grimace crossed her face.

Harrigan glanced at her; sighed. "Yup," he said. "Yup. Shultzy's box. Shultzy's papers."

Mabel Ryan's voice was thick: "Poor . . . Stan!"

The color was pouring out of Vivian's face.

Roy Stockland said, "Sit down, Vivian. I'll get you a drink of water." He led her to a chair and she sat down. Then he crossed the living room and disappeared in the bar.

Karen Langard was out of breath. "I can't, I can't believe it. I just *can't* believe it!"

I went over and stood beside Vivian. I wanted to say something to her but I didn't know what to say, so I just laid my hand on her shoulder. She reached up and took hold of my wrist. She held on tightly, her hand vibrating.

Harrigan said, "What's that?" He thrust the box into Mabel Ryan's hands and tramped toward the rear of the house.

"Sounded like a car starting," Hazelhurst said.

I heard a motor being raced, gears being clashed.

"Just a minute, Vivian," I said.

I ran through the bar, across the terrace, around the back of the house. Stockland had backed his car out. His rear wheels spouted bluestone splinters as he slammed it into first. The back door of the house flew open and Harrigan burst out.

I saw one of the guards coming on the run from the pavilion. I ran fast, as fast as I could, and made a dive for Stockland's running board. Harrigan had missed it and sprawled on the bluestone. I made it but Stockland struck with his left hand, sidewise, and caught me across the throat. I lost my balance, couldn't regain it, and jumped. I hit the lawn on my knees, then my elbows, and went head over heels.

Harrigan yelled, "Stop him! Stop that car!"

I sat up and saw the guard who had come from the pavilion run past. He had his gun in one hand, a whistle in the other. He blew the whistle. I jumped up and saw another guard down on the driveway where it entered the grove. He blew his whistle. He had a gun in his hand too.

I yelled, "Stop him!"

The guard at the beginning of the groved fired at the front tires but didn't hit them. He jumped out of the way and fired at the rear tires. But nothing happened. The car went lurching down through the grove. Both guards ran after it.

Harrigan came running up beside me. "It's okay," he said. "Hearing the whistles, the guys at the gate close the gate."

I ran along with him. In a minute there was a rasping metallic crash down in the grove.

Harrigan said, "The gates. Okay, kid. School's out."

He slowed down to a headlong walk and I walked along beside him down the driveway through the evergreens. In a couple of minutes we were able to see the iron gates. The car had sprung them when it hit but it had also turned over on its side, half way through. One of the guards was standing there craning his neck. I didn't see the other three but I heard sounds away on the left, in the trees.

Harrigan said, "Hey, what happened?"

"He jumped just before she hit," the guard at the gate said. "He run off. Ike went after him. Tom and Harry too."

"Didn't you try to stop him?"

"Sure. But I ain't going to shoot a guy unless it's me or him. Too many inquiries afterwards. And this guy ain't armed. I'm staying here in case they drive him back this way."

I turned and ran along a footpath that wound among trees and ferns. I heard Harrigan coming along behind me. Ahead, out of sight, someone yelled, "That way, Ike!" In a minute the path forked and I stopped and then Harrigan came up, pounding, and said, "Take that one, Webby, and I'll take this." He went left, so I went right.

In a couple of minutes I stopped and listened. There was a thrashing around in the woods near me somewhere, and I crouched down, waiting. Then one of the guards came jumping out of the bushes. I stood up and he almost fell over backward when he saw me. He pointed his gun at me and then lowered it.

He said, "Excuse me. For a second there I thought—"

"He must be pretty fast."

"He can run all right. Did he kill Shultz?"

"If he didn't, he's certainly creating a bad impression."

"I think I'll cut down this way."

He thrust off into the bushes and I ran on along the footpath. I came out in the open, a circular field where the sun boiled and you could smell the dry grass. Another guard was cutting along the opposite side. For an instant he paused to look at me, then ran on. When I entered the woods again I heard his feet pounding along up ahead. I came to another fork and sat down on a stump to get my wind, but a cloud of insects began circling around my head, so I got up and walked on.

At a turn in the path I found him sitting beneath a pine tree, holding his head in his hands. I stopped and said, "Hot work, isn't it?" He looked up without taking his hands from his head. There was a foggy expression in his eyes and his jaw was slack.

His voice lagged when he said, "Look out; he got my gun." His knees were flopped outward and he looked very tired. "I stopped to light a butt and he must ha' been standing behind this tree. He socked me with a rock, I guess. Look out; he's armed now."

"Are you hurt?"

"I don't think so. Just dizzy. I'll be okay. Only look out for him. Tell the others, if you see 'em."

I went along more cautiously now. Before, it was all right, but now it was different. Before, it was just a man with two hands but now it was a man with a gun. I heard sounds on the other side of a low ridge and stopped. I listened and heard the sound of voices.

"Harrigan," I yelled.

"Yeah?"

"He's got a gun." I climbed over the ridge and saw Harrigan standing with one of the guards. I said, "He clouted that big fellow with the yellow hair and got his gun."

"He must be nuts," Harrigan said.

A shot exploded in the woods down the slope. Its echoes clacked away among the trees and were smothered by two shots that were almost interlocked. The guard was crouched, his eyes popping. There were three shots in a row and their echoes clacked, then in a minute there was complete silence. Then a whistle blew.

"Blow yours," Harrigan said.

The guard blew.

A voice rose from the bottom of the slope. "Okay. Down this way. I got him."

We went down the slope. Stockland was sitting with his back propped against a tree. He didn't look up at us. His face was sweat-streaked, saturnine.

Harrigan said, "Who did all the shooting?"

"He did," the guard said. "Anyhow, most of it. I just fired once."

"Where'd you shoot him?"

"He ain't shot. When he emptied his gun I came out at him and just fired a shot at his feet, in front of him. I guess he's pretty tired, though. It's a hot day. Muggy."

CHAPTER XVII

I USED THE phone in the library to call Pascarella and as I hung up Mabel Ryan came to the doorway. She was holding the strongbox, which Harrigan had thrust into her hands.

She said, "This is probably dynamite. Will you take it?"

"I'll take it up to Harrigan, sure."

I went up to Harrigan's room and put the box down on his dresser. Stockland was sitting on a chair by the window. There were scratches on his face and arms from fighting through the bushes.

I said, "Pascarella says he'll be over in about twenty minutes."

Harrigan was taking it easy in a deep chair. "Well, the gun's his, all right," he said.

I looked at Stockland. He glanced over his shoulder at me and then stared out the window again.

Harrigan said, "When he went upstairs before to dress, after Mrs. Cantwell first said she was going to a hotel, he told her to take the gun and Shultzy's box in her bags."

"Where'd they been all along?"

"In a wall safe in Mrs. Cantwell's bedroom. He didn't have any chance to get them out of the house before. He made sure never to leave the house alone. That's so he wouldn't arouse suspicion."

"And then he runs out on Ivy?"

Stockland snapped across his shoulder, "I didn't run out on her. It was the only chance there was. She would have had to explain possession of the gun and Shultz's box and papers. Besides, when I bought the gun a year ago, its number was taken by the firm where I bought it. What would you have done?" he snapped.

"Run, I guess, the same as you."

He said in a bitter voice, "She took the gun about two weeks ago. From a compartment in my car. We were out riding. We stopped for some gas and I got out and while I was out she took it. I didn't discover it was gone until I got home. I'd told her that I didn't want to go on with her any longer, I was getting in too deep. And besides, I was preparing plans for Stan's new building. It was to have been one of the finest in the city. I didn't want that spoiled. But she took the gun and when I wanted it back she wouldn't give it to me."

He stood up and ground the knuckles of his right hand against the palm of his left.

Harrigan said, "Why wouldn't she give it back?"

"She said that if ever Stan came in her room, if he ever tried, she'd shoot him. And she had my gun. Friday afternoon I caught her in her room with the tray of her wall safe out on the bed. I tried to get the gun. She picked it up and I chased her around the room and she ran out in the hall. She ran into the first open room she came to and it was Hazelhurst's. She thrust the chair out of the way and tried to close the door but I got in and we struggled for the gun. It was in the struggle that the screen was knocked out. I had her by the open window, then, and in the struggle her hand, the one that held the gun, struck the sill and the gun went off and she dropped it. Shultz was down below, picking up the screen. He saw both of us. He picked up the gun too and walked back to the garage. Ivy ran back to her room. I went to mine and brushed up and then I went downstairs."

He turned and leaned straightarmed on the windowsill. "I accosted Shultz a couple of hours later and asked him for the gun. He wouldn't give it to me. He said he knew plenty about Ivy and me and that he was

going to tell Stan. I asked him to sleep on it and think it over. He said
he'd think about it."

He sat down and wiped perspiration from his face. "When we all
came home from the beach club Friday night, I couldn't sleep. I knew
he hadn't come home yet and I wanted to see him. I went downstairs at
about half-past two and looked in the garage and saw that the beach
wagon wasn't there. So I walked down to the gate and I was there when
he came along. He stopped and I asked him for the gun again. He didn't
answer. He simply put the car in gear but I reached in and knocked it
out. I grabbed hold of his arm, to talk to him, and he struck at me. I
struck back at him and then he picked up a short length of lead pipe
which I guess he carried on the seat for protection. I wrenched that
away from him and hit him on the head. I must have hit him very hard."

"Plenty," said Harrigan.

"Then I drove him to that gravel pit, put on his shoes, took his keys.
I threw the pipe in the river. I walked back here and unlocked his room
and pulled all the shades down. I had a flashlight shaped like a pencil
and I used it. Then I found the green strongbox but none of the keys
would open it. That was because there was a combination lock on it. I
shook it and I could tell there was something heavy inside. I put my
own shoes on, left his there, turned out my flashlight and pulled up the
shades the way they'd been before. Then I took the box to my room."

"Did you make that fake call?"

"Yes. From Ivy's room."

"How about Shultzy's bankbook?"

"It must have been on the floor all the time. Pascarella simply missed
it when he made his first search. Why should I have put it there when
my purpose was to help along the belief that Shultz was killed by someone far removed from this house?"

Harrigan wagged his head. "I can't understand why she didn't get a
divorce, if she couldn't stand him."

"She had no grounds. She kept inviting Mabel Ryan to the house in
the hope that she might eventually get some. She figured that if she kept
Stan away from herself, barred her door against him, he'd finally ask her
to divorce him. That way, she could ask for a larger settlement."

I said, "You certainly don't talk like a guy who was in love with her."

"I got caught," he said. "I got caught and I couldn't get away. She
wouldn't let me," He struck his knees. "And Stan was my friend."

Harrigan said, "I'm old-fashioned maybe, but any guy that monkeys
around with a pal's wife, even if she's willing, the guy's a heel."

Vivian was lying on a wicker long chair on the terrace. She moved her
legs over and I sat down on the edge of it. The twilight was soft and
had a sweet smell.

"What's Stan going to do?" I said.

"He's through with Ivy."

"Did he say so?"

"Yes. But I knew it before he said it. I know the exact moment it happened. When she came to after fainting, he was sitting on her bed bathing her face. I suppose that in the first moment of her consciousness she didn't remember what had taken place downstairs. She snatched the face cloth and threw it in his face. He got up and turned and walked out and right then I knew he was through."

"It took a long time, didn't it?"

"He'd built this dream around her and I guess he realized it was crumbling but he wouldn't admit it, even to himself. He wanted to take her away to the South Seas on that schooner he talked about. I guess he thought it might keep his dream alive. But she laughed at the idea."

"Maybe he'll go when this is all over."

She nodded. "I think he will. I think—you know, I shouldn't be surprised if some day he married Mabel Ryan. They've known each other since they were kids."

"Ivy never like Shultz, did she?"

"She was always trying to get Stan to fire him, but Stan wouldn't."

"Is her middle name Marie?"

"No. Her first name is Marie but she never used it. Ivy's her middle name."

"She used it when she was a kid in Rochester," I said. "That's where Shultz knew her. That's why she didn't want him around. That's why she refused to meet his brother."

She put her hands back of her head, closed her eyes. "I wish I could just say some magic word that would drive it all away, everything, all the nastiness and double dealing."

"Oh, it could have been worse."

"I don't see how."

"Sure. It could have dragged on and on. This way, it's all over."

She sighed. "I suppose so. You do make things sound logical."

"How would a guy go about making it sound logical that he's quietly nuts about some girl?"

"I think you could make almost anything sound logical."

"You're probably prejudiced in my favor."

"I'm afraid I am."

"Well," I said, "don't be afraid."

"I'm not afraid really."

"I wonder if we're both talking about the same thing."

She took hold of my hand. "I think so, Larry. I think so."

"You're certainly a mind reader."

"A girl would have to be, with you."

Fritz said that Harrigan was in the pantry and when I went in there, he was leaning with one arm on the refrigerator. The cook, Fritz's wife, was seated at the table.

"Well, first now," Harrigan said, "you cut up two pounds of chuck in inch cubes; you roll 'em in flour and then brown 'em in fat from a half a pound of salt pork. Then you cover the meat with boiling water and simmer it for an hour. Then you cut up, oh, about four carrots, four onions and a couple of green peppers, and then take a couple of bay leaves and whole cloves. Then you add two tablespoons of chili sauce and two tablespoons of chopped parsley and simmer a couple of more hours. Then you thicken the gravy and season to taste, we make it fairly hot, and then you serve it with Viennese noodles."

"My!" said the cook.

"Boy, it slays 'em!"

"And what do you call it, Mr. Harrigan?"

"We call it Viennese Potpourri. Yeah. And me an Irishman!"

THE END

SECRET CORRIDORS

By HUGH PENTECOST

THE WHOLE RYAN family, with the exception of Roger Ryan, was gathered in the living-room of the cool, dark house on East Sixty-third Street. Roger Ryan lay on the canopied four-poster in his bedroom upstairs, dead. He had been murdered. It was a fact which his family were trying to assimilate. That he was dead at all was hard enough to believe, though for a long time the threat of death had hung over him like a shadow. But murder, by someone who had shared the hospitality of this house, was too much to comprehend all at once. That was the other thing they knew and couldn't believe; it was one of them.

It was a strange kind of murder. There had been no violence, no gun, no poison. But for an accident it might never have been recognized as murder. Each member of the family, waiting there in the living-room, was thinking that perhaps it would have been better not to know.

The accident which had revealed the murder was literally an accident. A small boy who lived across the street had been throwing a ball up against the side of his house. The ball had escaped him and rolled out onto the street. He had run out to get it and been knocked kicking by a passing taxi. He had been carried into the house and a doctor sent for. The doctor happened to be Dr. John Smith. Dr. John Smith happened also to be Roger Ryan's physician.

The boy with the ball had not been badly hurt. Bruises and shock was the diagnosis. When Dr. Smith left the boy he glanced across the street at the gray stone Ryan house. He was not due to see Roger Ryan today, but since he was in the neighborhood he decided to drop in. He was received cheerfully by the housemaid. He knew his way about the house, and he went up and knocked on the door of Roger Ryan's bedroom. Getting no answer, he opened the door and went in, tiptoeing lest his patient be asleep.

Roger Ryan was not asleep. He was fighting a last violent struggle against death . . . fighting alone in silent agony. His white hair was

83

matted with sweat, his bony hands clutched despairingly at the bed covering. His eyes rolled wildly in their sockets.

Even before the doctor reached the bedside Roger Ryan drew one last strangling breath and lay still. When Smith's fingers found no pulse, the doctor called for help, but didn't wait for it to come. He had already administered a hypodermic when Lucille Ryan, Roger's daughter-in-law, answered his call.

There was nothing else to do except to wait without hope for a reaction to the hypodermic. It never came. While he waited, the doctor picked up a bottle of medicine from the bedside table. It was uncorked, and some of it had spilled on the table-top. The doctor raised the bottle to his nose and sniffed. He frowned. Then he cupped his left hand and poured some of the colorless liquid from the bottle into it. He tasted it with the tip of his tongue.

"God!" Dr. Smith said.

Not poison. Nothing more deadly than tap water. . . .

Inspector Bradley, sitting across the hearth from the little gray man, decided that at last he had found someone who could sign a hotel register "John Smith" and be believed. Dr. John Smith spoke in low, colorless tones. His clothes were a neutral gray. His face was as anonymous and undistinguished as his name. He was neither homely enough nor handsome enough to be noticed. He was neither tall nor short, not plump nor thin. He was, Bradley decided, the John Smith of all time.

But Dr. John Smith's negativeness ended with his exterior qualities. Bradley knew this after two hours of association with him.

"You have come to a conclusion, Inspector?" Dr. Smith asked.

"Yes."

"It's murder?"

"Yes," Bradley said without much expression. "I am thoroughly convinced of it."

"In a legal sense?"

"Definitely," Bradley said.

"What are you going to do?"

Bradley rumpled his close-cropped red hair. "Sweat!" he said, and his smile was crooked.

A log settled down on the fire, sending a shower of sparks up the chimney. The sudden light brought into focus the warm comfort and security of the book-lined study as compared to the April afternoon, which had turned raw with rain.

"A dead man and a four-ounce bottle of tap water," Bradley said. "Not a promising beginning."

"That tap water was as deadly as if someone had stood over Roger and slid a knife between his ribs," Dr. Smith said.

"I understand that," Bradley said. "I understand it too well. Look at it from my point of view, just as a problem, Doctor. If a man is killed by the proverbial blunt instrument, or a gun, I, the detective, start looking for that gun or blunt instrument. If he is poisoned, I start checking the sources of poison and those people who had access to the sources. But my investigation was over here in five minutes.

"Roger Ryan was killed because someone emptied out medicine that would have saved his life and substituted tap water for it. That tap water came from the bathroom eight feet away from his bed. Anybody in the house could have emptied the medicine and put water in the bottle. It was a process that left absolutely no incriminating traces. No definite fingerprints on the bottle, and it wouldn't be incriminating if there were. Everybody in the house has handled that bottle quite innocently. Same goes for the tap in the bathroom. End of investigation!"

"But the fact remains that it was cold-blooded and deliberate." Dr. Smith said. "Everyone knew that if Roger had a heart attack, all that stood between him and death was that medicine. The person who emptied it down the drain and substituted water for it knew that when Roger next had an attack—"

"I know, Doctor, I know," Bradley said wearily. "It's murder."

"The search for physical clues is really over before you begin," Dr. Smith said. "We have the bottle of water, but it doesn't tell us who did it and it never will."

"You're a comforting character, Doctor."

"It's a nice problem," Dr. Smith said. "A very nice problem."

"Oh, very nice, Doctor!" Bradley said. He reached out with the toe of his shoe and pushed, almost angrily, at the log on the fire. "We usually sew up a case from two angles. Physical clues point to someone, and then we find a motive. Q. E. D. All there is here is motive, since there are no pointing clues. . . . Tell me something about this family, Doctor, before I go talk to them."

Dr. Smith stared into the fire for a moment. "There was Roger," he said, "and there is Emily, his wife. There are three grown children, Bob, Julian, and Patricia. There is Julian's wife, Lucille. And there is Caroline."

"Caroline?"

"Miss Evans. She's Mrs. Ryan's sister. She's been part of this household for nearly thirty years, I gather. She runs things pretty much."

"Old maid?"

"Old maid," Dr. Smith said, "but not oldmaidish."

"And what are the others like?"

"You'd better form your own opinions, Inspector. I don't want to prejudice you."

"Okay, Doctor. One more thing: Do any motives suggest themselves to you?"

Dr. Smith was silent for a long time. "Nothing obvious," he said finally. "Not money, for example. A year ago, when Roger knew that he might die at any time, he distributed his money to the members of his family. They got their shares in his estate while he was still alive. In other words, there is nothing here like a will that might be altered to someone's disadvantage."

"No physical clues. No obvious motives. Nothing like revenge or jealousy, Doctor?"

"I don't know what those words mean," Dr. Smith said.

Bradley stared at him.

"Mr. Bradley, if a criminal kidnaps and murders a baby, and the baby's father catches up with the kidnapper and kills him, that's revenge. There has been a real wrong done, and the resulting pay-off is really revenge for that real wrong."

"I'll say it is!"

"But suppose the wrong is unreal," Dr. Smith said. "Suppose it is a fantasy in the mind of a person who only imagines he has been injured. Suppose, because of that fantasy, that person kills. Is that still revenge, Mr. Bradley? There has been no real wrong, so you cannot properly call it revenge."

"You're talking about metaphysical definitions, Dr. Smith. What have they to do with Roger Ryan's death?"

Dr. Smith was silent for a moment. "I don't want to give you my own impression of Roger Ryan as a man," he said. "Again, that would be prejudicial. But I don't think you are going to find a direct and obvious motive, Mr. Bradley. He has kidnapped no babies. In other words, no real or positive act of his drove someone to kill him."

"You mean the reason he was murdered is a fantasy reason and not a real reason?"

"Perhaps I'm riding a hobby," Dr. Smith said. "I have always believed that the motives ascribed to murderers are scarcely ever the real motives. The real motives lie deep and must be dug for. I think in this case you're going to have to dig."

"But surely, Doctor, some one of these people—"

"Let me draw you a picture," the doctor said. "You are crossing the street. The traffic lights are with you. A bus comes toward you down the street. You don't pay any attention to that bus because you know you have time to get across and that the bus will stop as it reaches the intersection. It represents absolutely no danger to you. Right?"

"Right."

"Suppose, however, that for some reason you were deprived of the function of walking, and that you had to crawl across the street on your hands and knees. From that position you see the bus approaching. It is no longer a matter of indifference to you. You're uncertain whether you

can cross the street in time. If you fail, the bus may run you down. It is
suddenly an instrument of destruction. Actually, Mr. Bradley, none of
the conditions have changed. It is still a bus and not a death-dealing
monster. But from your position on your hands and knees you can
never be convinced of that."

"And the point of this analogy, Doctor?"

"In the very complex human mechanism, Mr. Bradley, certain functions go sour. A person who is trying to use one of those non-working
functions suddenly sees everything from a distorted perception point.
To carry on the picture, you and I, functioning in a normal fashion,
may observe a man do something which we rightly diagnose as an act of
kindness. But someone else, functioning imperfectly, may see that same
action as threatening, as base, as treacherous."

"What you're getting at is—"

"What I'm getting at is this: I doubt if, in a straightaway investigation, you will discover a single action of Roger Ryan's which you, from
your normal perception point, will concede gave anyone the remotest
cause for murder. You will not find the motives on the surface, Mr.
Bradley. The motive lies somewhere in the dark and secret corridors of
the mind." . . .

The Ryans were still waiting in the living room. It was a high-ceil-
inged room with a black marble fireplace at one end. Family portraits,
gloomy and dark, stared down from the walls.

The rest of the room was a paradox. There were bright chintzes, comfortable over-stuffed furniture. It looked as if someone had moved
briskly into the room and set about the task of showing Roger Ryan's
stern-faced ancestors the advantage of modern as opposed to Victorian
furnishings. There was a low glass coffee table in front of the fire; a
bright chromium and red bar on wheels in the corner; gay, hand-
painted lamp shades.

In an old mansion off Fifth Avenue one might have expected something of whalebone and yellowing lace and high, winged collar about
its occupants; something dusty and formal. There was none of this.
There was a kind of sharp, astringent, dry-Martini brittleness about the
six people who waited.

Even Emily Ryan, the dead man's widow, had not quite caught the
mood of tragedy one might have expected. She wore a red-flowered
afternoon dress, a dress she always wore when there was to be a party in
the living-room. It went with the lamp shades.

"I suppose I should be wearing black," she said. She sat in a wing
chair by the fire. Her hands fluttered in her lap. Her hands always
fluttered. They were hands which had never been put to any other purpose than to be looked at and admired.

Caroline Evans, Emily's sister, said, "Nonsense, darling. Roger hated you in black." Caroline, herself, *was* in black, but very smart black. Her white hair was perfectly coiffed; little pearl ear buttons and a pearl necklace completed the picture of an extremely well turned-out business woman of fifty-five.

It just happened that Caroline's only business for thirty years had been running the Ryan household. Emily had no head for grocers' lists, or talking salary with servants, or organizing a system that ran smoothly and without the mechanics ever showing. Caroline not only could manage these things, but always gave the impression that she'd had nothing whatever to do with them.

Emily's three children did not seem greatly concerned with comforting her. Her oldest son, Bob, stood with his back to the fire, the heel of a custom-made shoe hooked over the fender. He was thirty. He had black hair and a small black mustache. Brown eyes were set widely in an expression of bland innocence. The expression seemed to say: "In spite of my slickness, the way I wear clothes, my man-about-town exterior, I am really a shy, kindly, inexperienced young man."

"I'll bet the old doc is giving that cop an earful about us," Bob Ryan said. He took a cigarette case from the pocket of his tweed coat and tapped a cigarette on the back of it. "What would I say if I were asked for a dossier on the family, I wonder?"

"What can Dr. Smith know to tell about us?" Emily asked.

"Dear Dr. Smith," Bob said scornfully. "Such a mouse of a little man —spelled with a capital L!"

"Dr. Smith's only done what he conceives to be his duty, Bob," Emily said. "Of course, he must be wrong." She looked around the room at the others, and her hands fluttered.

"We might as well face it, Mother," Patricia Ryan said. "He's not wrong."

"Patricia, how can you say that, dear? I mean . . ." Emily got no help from anyone else.

Patricia sat on the arm of the couch, swinging a leg. She wore a gray, pin-stripe suit with broad, padded shoulders. She had high cheekbones, a wide, red gash of a mouth, dark brown curly hair cut short. Her voice had a metallic quality. She jiggled the ice in her tall highball glass.

"Someone deliberately arranged for Father to die when he had his next attack. It worked, and it's murder. Why pretend? We're in for it, and we might as well face it."

"Really, Pat, I think at least on Mother's account you ought to—"

"Oh, for God's sake, Julian!" Pat said.

Julian Ryan sat on the couch with his wife, Lucille. He was holding her hand very tightly in his. Julian hadn't Bob's flair for wearing clothes. He always looked a little messy. Horn-rimmed glasses gave him an owlish expression which blurred the neat, chiseled arrangement of his face. His eyes were blue and vague like Emily's. His nose was straight, perfectly molded, just right. His mouth was straight, perfectly molded, just right. His voice wasn't plaintive; it was simply gentle and soothing.

"Pat's right, darling," Lucille Ryan said to her husband. Emily always turned her eyes on Lucille when Lucille spoke to Julian. "There's no point in ducking the facts. We're not going to be allowed to duck them."

Lucille was dark and attractive in a plain, straightforward fashion. "The typical earnest college graduate," Bob had called her. "A little thick in the soles of the shoe, very large in the heart, and, oh, so very damned direct!" She wasn't pretty enough to spend hours a day working at her prettiness, yet somehow she was very vitally feminine. Men liked her. Even Bob Ryan liked her. . . .

Of course, Lucille was right. They weren't going to be allowed to duck.

Bradley and Dr. Smith came into the living-room on the heels of a tea tray, wheeled in on a mahogany cart by a maid who had obviously been weeping. Bradley noticed that the maid was the only person present who had obviously been weeping.

Inspector Bradley was not exactly what the Ryan family had expected. There was nothing of the third-degree, back-room, rubber-hose aura about Luke Bradley. His manner suggested mildness, gentleness, patience. His gray eyes were deceptive. They looked at you with a sort of vague questioning, and then suddenly you were restive because they were boring straight at you.

Dr. Smith introduced each of the family in turn. They all seemed to be waiting for the detective to belch smoke and fire. It didn't happen. Bradley had a disconcerting capacity for stillness.

"Well, let's get started!" Bob Ryan said. "I suppose the first thing is alibis."

"Alibis for what, Mr. Ryan?" Bradley asked.

"Why—why, the time of the murder!"

"When was that?"

Bob stared at the detective. "Why, father died about four hours ago."

"I wish it was as easy as that," Bradley said. He sighed.

There was silence, broken by what seemed like a very loud noise. Dr. Smith was winding his watch.

Bob Ryan said, "There must be some critical time for which some of us can account."

"The critical time," Dr. Smith said unexpectedly, "probably was in the period when you were three or four years old, Bob."

"What are you talking about?" Bob asked.

Bradley took over. "I think I can make the situation clear to all of you," he said. "Roger Ryan's last attack was about two weeks ago. He took his medicine, and it was effective. The next he had was this afternoon. Again he took his medicine, but it wasn't effective, because someone had turned the medicine into water. You see where that leaves me. The substitution of the water can have taken place any time during the last two weeks. I can't begin to locate a critical time for that action—a time for alibis."

Julian looked up through his horn-rimmed glasses. He was holding Lucille's hand so tightly that his knuckles were white. "Aren't there fingerprints, or evidence of that sort?"

Bradley shook his head. He waited.

"Then what the blazes—" Bob began.

"The question, Mr. Ryan, is 'Why?' That's all we can look for."

"That's why I'm quite sure it's all a mistake," Emily said quickly. "My husband was a kind man, Inspector. Everyone in this household loved and respected him." She looked around at the others. "Isn't that so?"

"Of course it's so!" Pat said sharply.

"If Roger was murdered," Caroline Evans said quitely, "of course it's *not* so."

"Caroline!" Emily's voice was plaintive.

Caroline shrugged. "What's the use of pretending, Emily?"

Emily stood up. There was a kind of special dignity in the way she faced Bradley. "You are asking me to believe that one of my children—and I consider Lucille my daughter—or my sister, is a murderer, Mr. Bradley. I flatly refuse to believe any such thing or to consider it for a moment. Roger was ill. He might have died at any time. He—"

"Roger might have lived for ten years, Emily, with proper care," Dr. Smith said.

"Dr. John, you've always been our friend," Emily said, "and now you—"

"I was Roger's friend, too," Dr. Smith said, and looked straight at Emily. "I could understand and possibly even excuse a murder done in a fit of anger. Roger didn't die that way. The murderer arranged for him to die and was quite willing to wait patiently till the moment came. I must conclude from this that it was carefully considered and decided upon. The hatred or fear which led to such a crime, Emily, was built up over a long period of time. Mr. Bradley's task is to search for that hatred or fear and to find it in one of you."

Emily sank slowly back into her chair.

"Well, for God's sake let's get started and have it over with," Bob said. . . .

Lucille Ryan took a cigarette from a box on the study table. She fumbled with the lighter before she got it going. The investigation was about to begin, and for some reason she had been the first to be called into the study which Bradley had taken over as a headquarters. The detective was waiting for her to take one of the chairs beside the fireplace.

In the shadows of the room, over by the curtained windows, was Dr. Smith. He sat on a window seat, looking out at the driving rain. He was there, and yet he was not there. His intent seemed to be to efface himself.

Lucille sat down, and Bradley took the chair across the hearth from her.

"I really don't know why you've taken me first, Mr. Bradley," Lucille said. "I've only been in the family for eleven months. Julian and I were married just under a year ago."

"I like trying the easy things first," Bradley said, smiling. "You'd only known Roger Ryan a year. If you had any reason to kill him, Mrs. Ryan, that reason will be nearer the surface than in any of the others."

Lucille looked straight at him. "Of course I didn't kill him."

Bradley struck a match on the sole of his shoe and held it to the bowl of his pipe, squinting at her through the cloud of smoke.

"As a matter of fact, I was terribly fond of him," Lucille said. "He was my best friend, really, here in the house." There was still no help from Bradley, and she went on, her voice slightly raised: "That sounds as though I didn't get along with the others. That isn't true. I . . ." She stopped.

"Mother-in-law trouble?" Bradley asked.

"Not really trouble with Mrs. Ryan," Lucille said. "She's very sweet to me and she tries to keeps hands off Julian and me, but—"

"But Julian is stuck with her?"

"I can see you've been talking to Dr. Smith," Lucille said. She glanced toward the window seat. The doctor was still staring out at the rain.

"Dr. Smith refused to tell me anything about anybody," Bradley said. "But there is nothing the matter with my eyes and ears." He smiled again.

"Is it that obvious?" Lucille said. She crossed her legs, not bad legs. "It's not so much a problem with Mrs. Ryan as it is with Julian." She looked at Bradley and drew the corners of her mouth down in a wry expression. "I don't find it pleasant talking about the family to you, and yet I know it will all come out sooner or later."

"I'm afraid it will."

"I met Julian through my job," Lucille said. "When I graduated from college two years ago I got a job with the Raleigh Press. It's a book publishing house, you know. Julian is a junior partner. I got to be his secretary. He's terribly sweet and gentle and kind. We had a lot of things in common. We like to go to art galleries. We have much the same taste in books and in the theater and movies. It was fun going places with him. I don't like night-club splurging and neither does he. . . . Don't misunderstand me. Julian isn't tight about money at all. But we both feel that the things we want most in life are things you can't buy with money.

"Well, after six months of playing around together, it began to get serious, and finally Julian proposed to me. I was in love with him and I accepted. After we'd decided to marry, Julian brought me here for dinner one night.

"I felt like a horse at an auction at first." Lucille laughed a little. "They were all in the living-room to meet me—all but Father Ryan. Mrs. Ryan and Aunt Caroline were formally cordial and polite. Pat was a little hostile, I thought. And Bob—well, Bob seemed to be highly amused at the idea Julian had gotten any kind of girl for himself at all. I had the feeling that Bob and Pat thought good old Julian was suffering from the heat and that Mother Ryan and Aunt Caroline saw me strictly as some sort of dangerous intruder.

"Then Father Ryan appeared." Lucille's voice softened. "He came into the room in a wheel chair which he operated by himself. They'd built in an automatic elevator when his heart trouble developed, and he was able to get up and down that way without help.

"Mr. Bradley, it was like the sun breaking through the clouds on a rainy day when Father Ryan came into that room. It seemed to me he radiated warmth and kindness and understanding. He accepted me, without reservation, as one of them. And his presence seemed to affect the others. I was no longer the center of attention, and it made them seem different. Bob and Patricia and Mother Ryan and Aunt Caroline all seemed more outgoing. Only Julian didn't react positively in the presence of his father."

Lucille stopped, her eyes widening. "Mr. Bradley, please! You mustn't misunderstand that remark. Julian and his father were so much alike, only Father Ryan—how shall I say it? If you put two red colors beside each other, if one red has a brighter pigment it makes the other red look duller than it really is. As a matter of fact, I felt very good about Julian after I'd met Father Ryan. I could see what Julian might become when he'd gained a little more confidence in himself."

"Perhaps Julian resented being like his father and yet not quite so bright a red." It was Dr. Smith who spoke.

"No, no! He had the deepest respect and admiration for Father Ryan. There wasn't any rivalry between them."

Bradley was silent. He seemed suddenly to be concentrating on the stem of his pipe. Lucille went on. She was a little breathless now, as if she'd made a mistake she ought to rectify.

"It was Julian who really took over the management of things, although it was Bob's place as the oldest son. You see, a year ago Father Ryan distributed his estate to all his heirs. He said he didn't want any of us sitting around waiting for him to die. He said he expected to live for a long time, but . . ." She stopped, her voice unsteady. "When the estate was split up, it was agreed that the heirs who wanted to live here should all contribute their share to the running of this house. The heirs were Bob and Pat and Julian and Aunt Caroline.

"Of course, Father and Mother Ryan had their share, and now Father's share goes to her. It was really always hers. It was Julian who handled the financing of the household. I think Father Ryan was proud of the way he handled it, particularly in Bob's case. Getting money out of Bob is like getting blood out of rock. It's a matter of principle with Bob not to pay for anything if he can avoid it."

"Bob *is* tight with money?" Bradley asked.

"It isn't that," Lucille said. "It's just that—well, Bob has a curious quirk. If we play gin rummy and he loses twenty-five cents he'll forget to pay unless he's reminded. He's a crackajack golfer, one of the best in the Metropolitan area, and he doesn't need to cheat to win. Yet he can never quite add up his score correctly. Some people are like that, you know. There seems to be a sort of excitement in swindling people, even though you don't need to do it."

"I know the type," Bradley said.

"Pat's different. She's so honest it hurts. Julian's the same way, only with Julian it's natural and he makes no particular point of it. Pat never lets you forget. She's always pointing out the fact that she's met her obligations, as though we wouldn't believe it if we weren't told."

Lucille tossed her cigarette into the fire and lit a fresh one. "But I'm talking about the others instead of myself. After that first evening here, I was in and out of the house a good deal. But I have to admit, Mr. Bradley, that it never occured to me that when we were married we'd come here to live. I wanted my own home. But Julian made a great point of his father's illness. He said he was needed; that Bob wasn't a responsible person." She laughed ruefully. "I discovered a streak of stubbornness in Julian then that I hadn't known was there. I couldn't budge him. Well, he was my man and I wanted him on any terms, so I finally agreed."

"Decided to fight it out later?" Bradley suggested.

"That's quite true. I thought I could work on it gradually. But I discovered I had the wrong slant on it."

"Oh?"

"After we'd been here for a month I went to Father Ryan. I put my cards on the table. I told him I thought Julian and I should have a home of our own. I said I was sure he would understand and that the reason Julian was reluctant was on account of him.

"I'll never forget Father Ryan's face when I'd finished talking.

" 'You know, Lucille,' he said, 'I figured you had this situation more clearly in mind than you have.'

" 'I don't understand,' I said.

" 'Do you really think Julian insists on living here because of me?' He didn't sound hurt. He just sounded tired.

" 'I don't understand, Father,' I said.

" 'Lucille, boys grow up in all kinds of different ways. The average boy passes through infancy being dependent on both his mother and father, each for different things. Gradually he becomes independent and moves out on his own. But sometimes something goes wrong. It's not necessarily anyone's fault. The child focuses all his dependencies on one of the parents, usually the mother. When this kind of abnormal dependency is developed, it's the hardest thing in the world to get free of. Do you understand what I'm talking about, Lucille?'

" 'You mean that Julian and his mother . . .?'

" 'Yes, Lucille, I mean Julian and his mother. Julian never turned to me for anything. The bond between him and Emily is stronger than you imagine. I have tried to break it for Julian's own good. I couldn't do too much. In my position it would only seem to Julian that I was jealous. Emily, too, would have thought that. When Julian found the guts to ask a girl to marry him I was delighted. You're the right kind of girl, Lucille; the kind of girl who will help him to fight his way out of this. But don't underestimate the strength of his dependency. It's wound around like a—like a boa constrictor.' He looked at me and smiled sadly. 'Get your own place, Lucille, and get Julian into it—if you can. I'll be praying for you to succeed.'

"From then on I knew what I was fighting," Lucille continued. "I had a friend in Father Ryan, but it wasn't much use to me, except that I could go talk to him when the situation got too thick. You see, Mr. Bradley, living here, very few of the real functions of a wife fall to me. Aunt Caroline runs the house. All Julian's personal needs are taken care of in the ordinary course of running the house—what he eats, the care of his laundry, even the darning of his socks.

"That leaves almost no reason for my existence." A faint bitterness crept into her voice. "I sleep in the other twin bed! I try to be cheerful in the morning. I try to be cheerful when Julian gets home from the office. It's a kind of zombi-like existence. Julian insisted I give up my job, so I just have to *sit!*"

"And Julian doesn't recognize this?" Bradley asked.

"I've hinted at it. I said it straight out." Lucille laughed. "He's very patient with me. I just have to take it. If there is any sort of problem or question in his mind he turns to his mother, not to me. His concern for her comfort and happiness comes first. After that, if there's any time left for us, he's very generous with it. Oh, damn! I must sound horrible, but you have no idea, Mr. Bradley—"

"I think I have," Bradley said.

"Father Ryan saw the hopelessness of it," Lucille said. "Less than a week ago he made a move that was designed solely, I think, to help me out. He anounced he wanted to go to Florida. Dr. Smith had recommended sunshine and air. He suggested closing the house and actually putting it up for sale. His idea was that he and Mother Ryan would get a cottage for themselves in Florida, and the rest of us would go our separate ways. Everybody was independent financially, so there was no hitch on that score."

Bradley sat forward in his chair, his eyes suddenly quite bright. "You say he made this suggestion less than a week ago?"

"Yes."

"How did the others take it?"

In the corner, Dr. Smith turned his eyes away from the rain for the first time.

Lucille stared down at her hands, which were folded in her lap. "Bob and Pat seemed the least upset by the idea. I think Bob welcomed it. I think maybe it was the hardest of all for Aunt Caroline. She's given her whole life to the family. She'd be lost without this house to run."

"How did she happen to come to live with the Ryans, in the first place?" Bradley asked.

"I believe Mother Ryan was taken seriously ill very shortly after she and Father were married. Aunt Caroline came in to take charge until she got stronger. Then Bob was born, and she just stayed on."

"Did she raise any open objection to Mr. Ryan's idea?"

"Oh, no. She said she thought it was a splendid idea. She made some sort of joke about living alone and not knowing how to order for one person."

"And Mrs. Ryan?"

"I supposed she and Father must have talked it over, because she wasn't at all surprised when he brought it up. She seemed to think it was something Father ought to do, and obviously we couldn't all go trooping to Florida with them."

There was a moment of silence, and then Bradley said gently, "And Julian?"

Lucille's hands tightened in her lap. "Julian was dead set against it. He said if Father was so far away and he became seriously ill none of us would be on hand to help.

" 'We might as well face the fact, Julian, that one of these days I'm going to die,' Father said. 'Your being on hand won't speed or retard that process.' "

"And was anything decided?" Bradley asked.

"Nothing specific. But I know that Father had written to real-estate people in Florida."

"And what will happen now?" Bradley asked.

Lucille looked at him, and her lips quivered. "While I've been talking to you, Mr. Bradley, I suddenly realize that I'm scared out of my wits! With Father gone, I wonder if it will be possible to pry Julian away from his mother as long as she lives!"

"It'll probably be a tough job."

"God help me!" Lucille said. . . .

Dr. Smith came out of the shadows as Lucille left the study. "You have the beginnings of a portrait of Roger Ryan," he said. "Lucille's perception of the portrait. What does it look like to you, Inspector?"

Bradley thumbed through a small notebook in which he had been taking notes as Lucille talked. "He seems to have been a vital personality," he said, "kindly and understanding. He knew what the score was. His awareness of Lucille's and Julian's problem suggests he must also have been aware of the problems of the other people in the family. Does this check with your opinion of him, Doctor?"

"My opinion of him is not important," Dr. Smith said. "It's Lucille's perception and the perception of the others that's important."

"Do you think this projected breakup of the family could be a motive?"

"Possibly. If we knew what it really meant to each of them," Dr. Smith said.

"What about Caroline Evans? It hit her hard."

Dr. Smith shrugged.

"And Julian?" Bradley said. "It's fantastic to assume he would murder his father to keep his mother from moving to Florida. Or is it? Could his dependency be so strong he would commit murder to keep the umbilical cord intact?"

"I suggest you reserve your opinion of Julian until you've talked to him," Dr. Smith said. "What did you make of Lucille?"

"She seems straightforward and honest," Bradley said. "She's in love with Julian, but a little disappointed in him. She apparently had a real affection for Roger Ryan. She saw him as an ally. In those terms, his death is a blow to her chances of prying Julian loose from Emily. She does a pretty fair job of concealing what must be a deep hatred for Emily. There doesn't seem to be any motive in her case. She wanted Roger Ryan alive and active in her cause."

Dr. Smith nodded. "I agree," he said, "but I would like to call one singular fact to your attention."

Bradley looked up at him. "Yes?"

"When we first went into the living-room and you met the family, do you remember where Julian was sitting?"

"On the couch by Lucille."

"And hanging onto her hand for dear life!" Dr. Smith sighed. "It's odd he shouldn't have been closer to Emily and more protective. Is it possible his dependency on Emily is not as strong as Lucille imagines? If so, this would throw Lucille's whole story out of focus."

"Damn!" Bradley said softly. . . .

The Ryan family gathered in the dining-room. There were two extra and unoccupied places set at the table.

Caroline explained. "I thought we'd have to have Dr. John and the detective," she said. "Apparently we are to be allowed privacy. They've gone out for their dinner."

Bob emptied a highball glass he had brought in from the living-room. "You may not know it, dear family, but actually we're prisoners here." He was flushed, and his voice had a boisterous quality. "I tried to go out to get an evening paper, and found a flat-foot on the doorstep. Nobody leaves 'without the Inspector says so,' to quote the gentleman."

"He's been considerate, Bob," Lucille said. "I suppose we could all have been dragged off to some police station."

"I was looking you over," Bob said, "for the bruises from the night stick, but you seem to be all in one piece. What's Bradley getting at in these little heart-to-heart talks of his?"

Lucille looked down at her plate. "He wants to know how we felt about Father and about each other."

"And I suppose you told how you felt?"

"Yes."

"Dear little sister," Bob said. "I can feel the handcuffs over my wrists. Your account of me must have been a honey."

"Do shut up, Bob!" Pat said. "What was Lucille supposed to do, make you out a little plaster saint?"

"I wonder what she said about you, dear," Bob said. "Maybe she'll tell us."

"Bob, stop it!" Julian said sharply.

"Tattletale house," Bob said. "It's every man for himself, and let the dirt fall where it may."

There was a clatter as Pat's fork dropped on her plate. She pushed back her chair and stood up. Bright red spots had appeared on her high cheekbones. "Maybe the rest of you can stand this, but I can't! I can't just sit here and eat dinner and listen to Bob's wisecracks and know that one of you killed Father!"

"Patricia!" Emily protested.

"I'm sorry, Mother. I don't know how you can stand it, either. I don't know how you can sit there so calmly, knowing that one of us—"

"I don't know any such thing, Patricia! I don't believe it, and nothing will make me believe it."

"We have to believe it," Pat said. "There's no getting away from it."
She turned and almost ran out of the room.

There was a moment of complete silence. Then Bob said. "An excellent second act curtain." . . .

Julian took off his glasses and polished them carefully with a white
linen handkerchief. He was sitting in what had come to be the witness
chair in the book-lined study. He peered over at the window seat, where
Dr. Smith was almost hidden in the darkness.

Julian's manner was precise, and when he spoke it seemed to be a pre-
pared speech: "I wanted to thank you and Dr. John for not pouncing
down on mother immediately."

"We're trying not to pounce at all," Bradley said.

Julian put his glasses on again. "I don't quite know what you want
me tell you, or where you want me to begin."

"Begin anywhere, Mr. Ryan. I want to know about you—your relationship with your father and with the rest of your family."

"I see," Julian said.

He didn't seem to know what to do with his hands. First he put them
in coat pockets; then he brought them out and folded them in his lap.
"Father and I got along well," he said.

Bradley waited.

"We had our differences, of course," Julian said. "After all, we were
individuals. Unhappily, we were in disagreement over something at
the very time he died."

"The trip to Florida?" Bradley asked.

"Yes. I see Lucille has told you about that. It was a preposterous idea.
Father couldn't take care of himself. Mother isn't strong. She couldn't
have managed things for even a month without cracking up."

"Your mother's an invalid, Mr. Ryan?"

"Not exactly, but she's never been strong," Julian said. "She had a
very bad time when Bob was born. She's never really had her full quota
of strength since then. That's why Aunt Caroline came to live with us.
Mother never could have stood the double burden of bringing up the
children and running the house the way Father wanted it run."

"He had special requirements?"

"He liked people around, Mr. Bradley. Until his illness this was open
house to all his friends. We hardly ever sat down to dinner without
twelve or fourteen people. Running that kind of household was a full-
time job that Mother simply couldn't handle, with three of us to bring
up. I must say for Father that he didn't seem to expect it of her. It was
lucky he didn't and lucky there was Caroline."

"So your aunt became a fixture here at the time Bob was born?"

"I don't know exactly when. You see, Mother had Bob less than a year after her marriage. Caroline may have come toward the end of her confinement. Is it important to know exactly when?"

"Miss Evans can tell me that," Bradley said.

"The point I'm trying to make," Julian said, "is that Mother sacrificed her health in having us children. Father wanted a large family. I think he was disappointed when the doctors said Mother couldn't have another child after Pat. Sometimes I think he held it against Mother, though he must have realized, rationally, that it wasn't her fault."

"A man who's that fond of children must have been a good father," Bradley said.

"Oh, he was generous," said Julian, "and fair. He was something of a disciplinarian, but I *believe* in discipline. I think Bob was responsible for a lot of Father's sternness. Bob was never a very manageable kid, and Pat and I paid part of the price for it. Pat suffered from it worse than I did."

"Well, after all, Pat's a girl. But we were all brought up together, subjected to the same rules, and Father's attitude toward her was very much the same as his attitude toward Bob and me. The result of her getting exactly the same treatment is that she's grown up a tomboy. I know Mother tried everything she could to prevent it. It distresses her that Pat should have so few really feminine qualities.

"The worst of it was that, while it was his fault that Pat turned out the way she did, Father used to tease her about it. He'd ask her why she didn't bring beaux to the house. He was a great mimic, and he used to imitate the way she walked, and her mannerisms. I've heard her in her room crying, after Father had amused himself by teasing her."

Bradley's face was a study. "That sounds almost sadistic," he said.

"I don't think he meant to be cruel," Julian said quickly. "He just didn't stop to think. There were people he invited here whom Mother didn't like. She would speak to him about it, but he never seemed to pay any attention. The same people would turn up again. I think it was just thoughtlessness. Quite naturally, he liked the people who responded most to his own particular kind of charm. These people who loved Father were very apt to pass Mother by, almost as if she didn't exist. I repeat, I don't think Father ever meant to be unkind to Mother. It was just that he was an egotist; he enjoyed applause. I think that explains his teasing of Pat. The rest of us were an audience and we used to laugh unthinkingly."

"What about your own relationship with him?" Bradley asked.

"I don't remember much about Father till I was, roughly, four. Pat had been born then. We three kids lived in the nursery upstairs. We didn't see much of father except when he came in to say good morning and good night.

"Of course, we saw Mother all the time. There was a nurse, but Mother never left us to her. She used to read aloud to us and sing us songs, and it was always she who took us to the park for our outdoors. In the summers we used to go to the country, and then we'd only see Father week ends. It's perfectly natural, in those conditions, that I should have been closer to Mother than I was to him.

"It was different with Bob. He was always rebellious—always scheming to find some way to get what he wanted. Mother just couldn't handle him. That left it up to Father. The result was a kind of duel that went on between Bob and Father right up to now. Bob was always trying to find a way to get what he wanted and skip the punishment for it. Father was always right on his tail, and almost always caught Bob out.

"It was almost like a game. He and Bob would actually laugh together when Bob was caught out. Then Bob would have to pay the piper."

"Spankings?" Bradley asked, very casually.

"No, the punishments were that he had to go without something he wanted or some privilege. Bob was always in the doghouse."

"What about you? Did you run up against the same kind of discipline?"

"Occasionally, when I had it coming to me. I say, again, Father was entirely fair when it came to that sort of thing." Julian rolled up his tie and then unrolled it. "Father was a great outdoor man. He loved to play golf, loved to fish. He liked all kinds of competitive games. I never was fond of them. Maybe that's because Bob was always better at them than I was. Even Pat was better. I'm just not the kind of guy, I guess. I've always liked to read. I liked mechanical toys as a kid. I've always loved puzzles. As a youngster I thought I wanted to be a civil engineer."

"Were you interested in ships?" The question came from the window seat.

Julian peered over at the corner toward Dr. Smith. "As a matter of fact, I hated ships."

Bradley looked puzzled both by the question and by the answer.

"Shipping was Father's business." Julian explained. "Imports and exports."

"Did your father want you to go into the business?" Bradley asked.

"I suppose it would have pleased him if one of us had. Bob, of course, has never done work of any kind. Father didn't raise a row about it, if that's what you mean."

"You finally went into the book publishing business," Bradley said.

"Yes. I guess I really like more to read and to hear about things than to do them. The engineering bug died early. I liked home. I didn't want to go places."

"Apparently you didn't want a home of your own, though," Bradley said.

Julian laughed outright. "Poor old Lucille! She's given you her song and dance about my not wanting a place for us. It was obviously necessary for me to stay here. Father was desperately ill and Mother not strong. If one could count on Bob . . ." He shrugged.

"Will you take a place of your own now?"

Julian frowned. "I don't know," he said. "I don't know. It depends a good deal on Mother." He looked at Bradley, his eyes suddenly wide and a little frightened. "If you and Dr. John are right, that means somebody else—some one of us—is going to be lost to Mother. I don't know if she'll stand up under it." He wriggled unhappily in his chair.

"Did you murder your father, Mr. Ryan?" Bradley asked abruptly.

Julian jumped to his feet. "Good heavens, man, *no!*" . . .

Dr. Smith and Bradley were alone, facing each other across the hearth. The doctor's voice was expressionless as he asked, "And what about your portrait of Roger Ryan now, Inspector?"

"Blurred," Bradley said, "to put it mildly. According to Julian, he was an egomaniac, thoughtless, even sadistically cruel. He was vain, applause-loving. The only really plus quality Julian gives him is a kind of rigid fairness."

"Lucille's story is almost totally white," Dr. Smith said. "Julian's almost totally black."

"It certainly bears out your theory, Doctor. Here are two entirely different perceptions of Roger Ryan. Lucille calls him aware, thoughtful, kind. Julian calls him unaware, thoughtless, cruel."

"And what did you think of Julian?" Dr. Smith asked.

"He's introspective," Bradley said, "Afraid of competition, either with his father, brother, or sister. He likes to read and hear about things, but not do them. Yet he has a streak of almost mulish stubbornness."

"It would be interesting," Dr. Smith said, "to know whether this stubbornness shows itself anywhere else than when an effort is made to pry him loose from the imagined security of his mother and his mother's home. And there's another important angle to his story, I think."

"Yes?"

"According to him, his father's cruelty, real or imagined, was only leveled at his mother and sister. He never once suggested that Roger was cruel to him or Bob. Is it possible that, since in his mind his father's sadism was directed only at women, he conceived that Lucille, who had grown close to Roger, was in danger? Or did he imagine his mother would be in danger of some kind of violence at Roger's hands if she were forced to live alone with him in Florida? Either of these fantasies *could* be a motive for murder, Inspector."

"That young man is mixed up enough to bear definite watching," Bradley said. . . .

Julian opened the door of his bedroom and went in. Lucille was sitting in front of the dressing table, wearing a negligee. She was brushing her dark hair.

Julian closed the door. "Well, they've gone for the night," he said.

Lucille turned to him, "Did you have a bad time, darling?"

"No."

"Julian, there's no doubt about this, you know."

"I know."

"Julian, you don't suspect me, do you?"

"Good heavens, no," Julian said.

"I don't suspect you," Lucille said, quite seriously.

"I should hope not." Julian took off his coat and hung it in the closet. "Somehow, I'm like Mother. I can't get it through my head. You can't escape the facts, and yet in a way I don't believe them."

"I believe them," Lucille said.

"But, Lucille, surely you can't think that Bob or Pat or Caroline could do a thing like this."

"Or your mother," said Lucille, looking very hard at herself in the mirror.

"Lucille! That's a hysterical and irresponsible statement! You don't like Mother. You—"

"Julian?"

"What?"

"If I asked you to do something odd would you do it?"

"I don't know, Lucille. What is it?"

"Would you lock our bedroom door tonight?" . . .

Shortly after eight-thirty the next morning the housemaid admitted Bradley to the Ryan house.

"The family's still at breakfast, sir," she said.

"Let them finish," Bradley said. "When they have, ask Miss Patricia if she'll come into the study."

"Yes, sir."

There was a fire going in the book-lined room and Bradley walked over to it.

"I trust you slept well, Inspector."

Bradley turned. Dr. Smith seemed to have materialized from behind the draperies at the window.

"I didn't see you," Bradley said.

"I was thinking," Dr. Smith said.

The study door opened and Pat Ryan came in. She wore a canary-yellow sweater and a herringbone tweed skirt. If anything, the red of her mouth was brighter, the tilt of her chin more defiant, than Bradley remembered it.

"You're an early bird," she said. "Hi, Dr. John. You, too?"

"You seem to have slept well," The doctor said.

"What nature won't do a sleeping pill will," Pat said. She took the chair the others had sat in, across the hearth from Bradley. Then she squirmed around in it to look at Dr. Smith, who had retired to the window seat. "Do you have to hide, Dr. John?"

The doctor didn't answer. He sat on the window seat, hands resting on his knees, his eyes apparently studying the intricacies of the rug pattern.

"Well, it's not very cozy," Pat said.

"We're not embarked on a cozy business, Miss Ryan," Bradley said. "I want you to tell me about your father. I want you to tell me what sort of a person he was, what your own relationship with him was."

Pat turned in the chair again. "If you're looking for a hatred of Father or a fear of him in me you're not going to find it, Mr. Bradley. Ask me what you want to know." She took a package of cigarettes from the pocket of her skirt, lit one, and then swung her legs over the arm of the chair.

"Were you fond of your father, Miss Ryan?" Bradley asked.

"I loved him with all my heart."

"You got along with him?"

"Perfectly."

"As a little girl, you were brought up along with Bob and Julian without any special differentiation because you were a girl?"

"How else are children brought up? They eat the same food, they have to be house-broken in the same way, they learn to walk and think. If you're trying to find out if I played with dolls, the answer is yes. Bob and Julian didn't. That's a difference." Then she laughed. "Julian did have to have a Teddy bear to go to sleep with until he was fourteen."

"About discipline," Bradley said. "Was your father pretty firm-handed?"

"He was firm with Bob. You have to be if you don't want to lose your gold inlays."

"But you didn't have the feeling your father was unusually stern?"

Pat laughed. "He was a lamb! We're born into a certain kind of society and we have to learn to function in it. There's no use crabbing about. That was Father's theory?"

"So there was no iron hand?"

"Not if you behaved in a halfway civilized fashion. Then most of the iron was in Mother. You could argue with Father, and if there was any reason or justice on your side, he'd concede. Mother has always been arbitrary."

"Was this particularly her attitude toward you, Miss Ryan, or did she treat Julian and Bob the same way?"

"She gave up on Bob early in the game," Pat said. "Bob was Father's cross. Julian's always been a mouse, so he simply did what Mother said, without question. I've always had arguments with her. She *did* try to treat me differently from the boys. I wasn't supposed to read certain books they were allowed to read or see certain movies they were allowed to see. I've always been shushed if I used the kind of language they used. 'Nice young girls don't talk that way, dear.' " Pat's imitation of her mother's voice was perfect.

Bradley took his pipe from his pocket and began to fill it. "You seem to have you father's talent for mimicry," he said.

"Father was wonderful at that sort of thing," Pat said. "He could imitate all of us to a T. He used to keep us perpetually amused that way when we were children."

Bradley put his pipe between his teeth. "Did it always amuse you?"

"Unfailingly."

"You were never upset when he happened to imitate you?"

"Good Lord, no. You couldn't be hurt by it! It was the gentlest kind of kidding. As children, we almost took it as a favor when he chose to imitate one of us."

"And when you grew up?"

"Look; I don't get this," Pat said. "Father was gay and amusing. I can take a ribbing, particularly when it's a clever one."

"It would save time if you'd tell us the truth, Pat." Dr. Smith said. He'd shifted his attention to the gray plaster walls, and kept it focused there even when Pat whirled around.

"Just what do you mean by that, Dr. John?"

"He means," Bradley said gently, "that your story doesn't check with what we've already heard. We've been led to believe that your father's 'ribbing,' as you call it, had a definite flavor of cruelty about it. We've been led to believe that he chided you about your tomboyish qualities, about not having beaux."

"Blast and damn Julian to hell!" Pat blazed. "He's always been a nosy, talebearing—"

"If you weren't hurt, Pat," Dr. Smith interrupted quietly, "why did you cry when your father imitated you?"

"I didn't cry when he imitated me!"

Bradley was silent.

"I tell you I *didn't!*" Pat repeated.

Bradley remained quite still for a moment and then, before he could reopen his questioning, Caroline Evans came into the study. She still wore black. She was still chic, perfectly turned out, but her face had no color to it at all and her lips were drawn together in a thin line. She crossed the room swiftly, to stand in front of Pat's chair.

"You miserable little vandal!" she said.

"Aunt Caroline!" Pat's eyes were wide with amazement.

Caroline Evans held a piece of crumpled newspaper in her hands. She rolled it open and held it out for Pat to see. She was carrying something in it. Bradley stood up and looked over her shoulder. In the newspaper, were hundreds of small pieces of torn white paper.

"What is it?" Pat asked.

"Don't give me that baby-faced stare," Caroline said. "You know what it is."

"But, Aunt Caroline, I don't!"

"It's what's left of the collection of lithographs your mother and father made together! The maid found them in the wastebasket in your mother's upstairs sitting-room. These are only part of the scraps you left."

"But, Caroline, are you accusing me of—?"

"Who else could have made this kind of vicious attack on your mother? You know what this collection meant to her."

"But I tell you—!" Pat cried.

"I think perhaps you'd better explain this, Miss Evans," Bradley said.

"I'll explain it," Caroline said. She was still biting off her words in separated, clipped syllables. "My sister has never been very strong. There weren't many things she and Roger could do together. She isn't fond of games. Over the years they've made a collection of lithographs of famous sailing ships. They were particularly precious to Emily because they represented time spent together."

She paused to draw a deep breath. "Last night somebody went into Emily's upstairs sitting-room, where these lithographs were kept in folios. They took out every one of them and tore them into tiny shreds, as you can see here." She literally jammed the newspaper under Bradley's nose. "It's a cruel and malicious act. First Roger is taken away from her, and then the closest and most personal link she had with him is destroyed."

"And you're accusing Miss Ryan?"

"Why not!" Caroline turned the fury of her gaze on Pat. "You've always hated your mother, Patricia. You hated her because she could take five minutes of your father's time from you. You hated her because she came first with your father. You hated her—"

"Shut up!" Pat shouted. She was on her feet, her hands clenched at her side.

"You've always been vindictive!" Caroline went on mercilessly. "You've always hated anyone who—"

Pat launched herself at her aunt, fingers bent like sharp claws. But those fingers only dug into the shoulders of Bradley's tweed coat, for somehow the detective was suddenly between the two women.

"Sit down," he said gently.

"She can't say those things!"

"Sit down!"

Pat sank into the chair, hunched together like a tensed spring. A hand dropped quietly on her shoulder and gave it a squeeze. The hand belonged to Dr. Smith.

"The destruction of these lithographs may be a very important part of this case, Miss Evans," Bradley said to Caroline. "Who else knows about it?"

"No one but Sally, the housemaid. I don't want Emily to know. It's the kind of thing that might tip her completely off balance at the moment."

"Have the maid keep quiet about it." Bradley said. "And don't talk about it yourself to anyone."

"What are you going to do about it?" Caroline asked. "She must be punished for this, Mr. Bradley. I can tell you in detail why she did it. I can tell you things—"

"You'll have the chance later," Bradley said. "In the meantime, be good enough to wait outside."

Caroline stood staring down at Pat for a moment, then turned and walked out.

Neither Bradley nor Dr. Smith broke the silence that followed. Pat was still hunched up in the chair, her teeth fastened over her lower lip. Then, slowly, she relaxed. At last her head dropped back against the chair and her eyelids closed. From beneath them two large tears ran down her pale cheeks. She made no effort to hide them. Bradley and Dr. Smith exchanged a glance, then the doctor walked softly over to the window seat. Bradley turned his back on Pat and went through the elaborate business of filling and lighting his pipe.

"Okay," Pat said at last. "Okay. I've finished with bawling."

Bradley sat down opposite her. His eyes told her nothing, asked nothing.

"I didn't touch the lithographs," Pat said. "I've never touched them. I never even looked at them in my life. Caroline's right. I resented them and what they stood for. She's also right about Mother. I hate her."

Bradley didn't speak.

"I told you I didn't cry when Father teased me," Pat said. "That was only partly true. I didn't cry *because* he teased me. He could have teased me or beaten me or run over me with a steam roller, and I'd have been grateful for that much attention. But I *did* cry. I cried because I had to share him with everyone—with everyone in the world, it seemed. I cried because I had to use all kinds of tricks and shams to get his attention. I was just another one of his kids to him. He couldn't see that he represented everything romantic and adventurous and glittering in the world to me.

"I couldn't tell him when he asked me why I didn't have beaux, that he, himself, was a yardstick against which nobody could measure. I couldn't tell him that I only wanted to be with him."

Pat covered her eyes with her hands. Then after a moment she let her hands drop back into her lap.

"I like parties. I like fun. I like pretty clothes and a good time. But I wanted to go to parties with Father. I wanted my fun with him. If I'd shown I wanted to go places with him they'd have made me go with someone else.

"He liked games, so I learned to play games. He liked golf and swimming and sailing and fishing. I became good at all those things because it meant I could be with him without spoiling his fun. He and Bob were always quarreling, and Julian never liked anything Father liked. He took me to Canada on a fishing trip once. 'You know, Pat,' he said, 'you give me all the pleasure I always thought I'd get from Bob and Julian. It's very swell for me, darling, but I wonder about you.'

"I couldn't tell him to stop wondering; that being with him made me happier than anything else in the world could make me.

"Mother was always frail. She could never do any of the things he would have liked to have her do with him. It wasn't her fault, but I hated her for it. I hated her for letting him down. He wanted so much from their life together that she couldn't give him. She just couldn't give it. He was so kind and so patient and so thoughtful of her. I've known, innumerable times, of his phoning people after he'd invited them to the house, saying it was all off because Mother wasn't well. He tried to sense her moods. He racked his brains to think of things that would be fun for her to do."

"Did he know how you felt, Pat?" Dr. Smith asked gently.

"If he did, he never showed it. He seemed to take our relationship for granted—quite naturally, I suppose. I never put it into words before, myself. But I had to do it after Caroline came in here, hinting that I—" She hesitated a moment. "I've never gotten on well with Caroline or Mother. It was because I wanted to do the things for Father they did. I wanted to run his house. I wanted to be his hostess."

Pat took a compact from her pocket and repaired the damage to her face. Her chin was up in the old, defiant manner when she looked at Bradley again. "I don't know who killed Father, but, whoever it was, I'll attend his execution with pleasure!" . . .

"There are people who love so much they can't bear to share the object of that love with anyone. They would rather see the loved one dead," Dr. Smith said.

Bradley leaned back in his chair. "I don't think I was ever so sorry for anyone in my life. I'd hate to have to pin it on her."

"We can't pin it on anyone yet," the doctor said. "But we can't dawdle, Bradley. The destruction of those lithographs distresses me. It is a kind of assassination, not very different from murder. Our killer is still in a dangerous mood."

"We'll check the upstairs sitting-room," Bradley said. "There's an outside chance there may be some sort of physical clue lying around at last. Perhaps fingerprints."

"Don't count on it," Dr. Smith said gloomily.

Bradley went out to consult with one of his men. He came back in about five minutes. Dr. Smith seemed not to have moved since he left.

"The portrait grows," he said, as if he had been talking right along. "We're back on the white side again—kindliness, thoughtfulness, consideration."

"Some doubt cast on Roger Ryan's awareness, though," Bradley said. "If he didn't know about Pat."

"We don't know if he knew or not," the doctor said. "But there are additions. Pat paints him as man with deep frustrations—frustrations in his relationship with Emily, frustrations in his relationships with his sons."

"Pat seems to have been pretty much in the same boat herself."

"Yes. Frustration. A bad frustration. I hope she can work her way out of it. But you see, Bradley, there is magic in her perception of her father. A magic that made him the most wonderful, the most sensitive, the most complete person in the world. Suppose—just suppose—that some act of Roger Ryan's destroyed that magic picture of himself. You see what would happen then, don't you?"

"Disillusionment," Bradley said.

"Something more like the *real* Roger Ryan destroying the *magic* Roger Ryan. And what might Pat's reaction be in that case? She would suddenly hate the real Roger Ryan passionately for doing away with the magic Roger Ryan. She might," Dr. Smith concluded, in a very small voice, "even murder the real Roger Ryan to revenge her magic Prince Charming, now gone forever." . . .

Bob Ryan stood at the bottom of the stairway in the main entrance hall. He was looking upward to the second-floor hallway, looking and listening. He carried a cigarette in one hand and a highball glass in the other.

Lucille came out of the living-room and paused at the foot of the stairs to speak to Bob.

"Pretty early for highballs, isn't it, Bob? It's only ten-thirty."

"Darling, I have never found a time that was too early or too late for highballs," Bob said. "It is always just exactly the right time."

"You look as though you were up to something," Lucille said.

"I yearn to talk to the masterminds," Bob said. "Suddenly it becomes urgent for me to spill out the contents of my little heart for them." He kept his eyes raised to the second-floor hallway.

"What's going on up there?" Lucille asked.

"The masterminds are in Mother's private sitting-room."

"Whatever for?"

"They're looking for clues, darling." Bob smiled blandly at her. "Did you leave any?"

"What are you talking about?"

"Hasn't the news trickled through to you yet?" Bob laughed. "Ask Julian."

"I certainly will," Lucille said, and started up the stairs.

She was halfway up when Bradley and Dr. Smith appeared and started down. They said good morning, politely, but did not stop to talk to her. They didn't seem inclined to talk to Bob, either. Bob had other ideas.

"Any clues to the vandal?" Bob asked.

Bradley looked at him sharply. "What vandal?"

"Now, really, Inspector, you don't think secrets can be kept from me in this house. Unearthing secrets is my lifework, you know. Did the person who destroyed Mother's lithographs leave his trade-mark?"

"Who told you about the lithographs?"

"A little bird," Bob said. "And I don't have to be a detective to know who did it."

"I had meant to delay the extraordinary pleasure of talking to you, Mr. Ryan," Bradley said dryly. "However, since you seem to know all the answers, that would be a tactical blunder. Come into the study."

"At last," Bob drawled, "the mysteries of police procedure are about to be unveiled."

He strolled over to the fireplace, put his glass down on the mantel, and stood with his back to the fire. "Do I begin or do you begin?" he said.

"You do," Bradley said. "And I don't intend wasting much time with you, Ryan. I don't expect you to tell me the truth, and I don't intend spending much time listening to anything else."

"I like that!" Bob laughed, unabashed. He crossed over and plopped down into the big armchair. "My precious family must have done a really swell job on me. . . . Oh, well, I came here to tell you who tore up the lithographs, and I will. It was Caroline, of course."

"Miss Evans?"

"In person," Bob said. "Masterful performance she must have put on, accusing Pat."

"How do you know she did it, and how do you know she accused your sister?" Bradley asked.

"I know she did it because I am an intelligent and observant person. I know she accused Pat because she told me she had."

"She told you?"

"Yes," Bob said. "Oh, I know it was against your orders, Inspector, but Caroline just can't keep anything from me."

"Does your personal charm account for that, Ryan?"

"A certain kind of charm," Bob said.

"That certain kind of charm wouldn't be blackmail, would it?" Bradley asked sharply.

"That would be rather a tough word for it," Bob said.

"And were you able to blackmail her into an admission that she tore up the lithographs?"

"Even my powers failed me there," Bob said. "I confess I tried it and failed."

"But you know she did it?"

"But of course." Bob spread his hands to indicate it was obvious. "Now, it couldn't be me, because the lithographs were worth money! It couldn't be Lucille; she's too pure and sweet. It couldn't be Julian. He might dream of doing it, but Julian never acts. Obviously, it wasn't Mother. That leaves Pat and Caroline. I happen to know it wasn't Pat."

"How do you know that?"

"Because Pat made a scene at dinner last night and stormed out of the place. When I went up to bed I saw a light shining under her door. I went into her room to tell her she'd behaved like a jerk. She was asleep with the light burning. The book she'd been reading had fallen on the floor. I tried to wake her up and couldn't. Then I saw the bottle of sleeping tablets. She was out like a light. I heard Lucille trying to wake her at breakfast time. She was still slug-nutty." Bob sighed. "But that isn't the real reason I know it was Caroline."

"I'm waiting," Bradley said.

"I know she did it because she was in love with Father," Bob said. "She always has been. I know it because I came across some letters she'd written Father before he was married."

"How did you 'come across' them?"

"I found them," Bob said.

"Where?"

"She kept them in a tin lock box."

"A lock box suggests a lock, Mr. Ryan."

Bob grinned disarmingly. "I *did* have to pry it open," he said. "Of course, I was only about ten. Those letters were hot stuff. It seems Caroline was pretty sore when Father decided it was Mother he wanted. She apparently had the idea that she held the lucky number. She's been sitting here for thirty years eating out her heart while Father lived his life with Mother. I don't know if you realize just how important those lithographs were to Mother."

"How important?"

"It wasn't the lithographs themselves," Bob said. "But Father made a great point of the collection. He and Mother went off on expeditions together to print shops and dealers. These expeditions involved tea and a ride in the park in an open victoria. It was really Father's way of making love.

"That's why they mean so much. They were a symbol of a special privacy, a special intimacy. The sight of them must have shriveled Caroline's soul. She wanted that privacy, that intimacy, for herself. For all I know, she may have murdered Father because he planned to go away and turn her out to pasture, as it were."

Bob looked at Bradley, smugly satisfied.

The distaste Bradley felt was carefully hidden. "It's an interesting theory, at any rate, Ryan. Now tell me something about yourself and your own relationship with your father."

"There's nothing much to tell," Bob drawled. "It was a sort of thirty-years war. We never saw eye to eye about what I should do or have. I got what I could for myself. Sometimes I got away with it and sometimes I didn't. Sometimes I let myself be caught doing something I wasn't supposed to do, so Father would be sure to keep on thinking he was pretty smart. It's always better to let the other fellow believe he's cleverer than he really is."

"You were fond of your father in spite of your disagreements?" Bradley asked.

"There was a kind of blundering sweetness about him," Bob said. "He never really knew what was going on around the place."

"But you knew. You made it your business and used it profitably, like Caroline's letters," Bradley said. "Blackmail seems to have been a racket of yours."

"I still think that's a tough way to put it," Bob said. "Everybody uses what they know about people in their relations with them."

There was sudden movement behind Bob's chair. Dr. Smith came over from the window seat, rather swiftly. "There's not much point in questioning him, Inspector, He won't talk except to exhibit his own remarkable shrewdness. But I'd like to talk for a minute if you don't mind."

"Of course," Bradley said. "Take over."

Dr. Smith turned to Bob. There was a pale and angry light in his eyes. "I'm going to tell you, Bob," he said, "what makes you a cheat, a liar, and a thief."

"Oh, come now, Dr. John!"

"Because that's what you are, Bob." The doctor's voice remained colorless, but as he spoke it grew gradually louder and louder until it filled the room. "You are a cheat, a liar, and a thief because of an enormous greed—a greed to acquire the whole universe for yourself! You hate your mother, your aunt, and your sister and brother because they're sharing your father's money. You want it *all* for yourself! You hate them when they eat the food that's brought on the table. You want it *all* for yourself.

"You hate us here in this room because we talked to some of the others first. We should have known that *you* are the only person who should be questioned, that *you* have all answers. You hated your father because he denied you things. He had no right to deny you things, because they were *all* rightfully yours. And since no one can acquire everything in the world for himself by honest means, you have to resort to lying, and cheating, and stealing, and treachery!

"I can paint your picture of your father for the Inspector. A miser, holding back what was rightfully yours. A villian who stood between you and satisfaction of your hunger! A treacherous enemy who deliberately, and before your very eyes, passed along some of the world's goods to your mother, your aunt, your sister and brother. In your eyes, Bob, your father must have been a fiend!"

The little doctor was breathing hard as he finished. Bob just stared at him. There was perspiration on his forehead.

"I don't know whether you killed him," Dr. Smith said, his voice quiet once more. "I don't know whether you killed him because he denied you something or because he had always denied you *everything!* I know you *could* have killed him. We'll have to wait and see. The facts are not all in. Now, get out!" . . .

"I'm sorry," Dr. Smith said. "I guess I talked too much."

"My dear Doctor, you were superb," Bradley said.

"I knew there was no point in questioning him. He would never say what he felt, because what he feel is so monstrous."

"You've observed him here in your visits?"

"His isn't an unusual case," Dr. Smith said. "It required no special powers of observation. It often happens with the first child in a family. For the first year or so in his life all he had to do is squawk and he *gets* the whole world, which at that time is food, clean diapers, and sleep! He comes to believe that he can have anything he wants for the asking. He gets all his parents' attention. Then the second child is born. Some children adjust to this. They learn that they must share with others.

"Other children, like Bob, don't adjust. They still think they are entitled to everything. So they begin to steal, to plot, to scheme, for what they imagine is rightfully theirs."

"And you think he could kill?"

"I think he could. I don't say I think he did. I don't know." . . .

Bradley had one very definite impression of Caroline Evans as she sat across the hearth from him in the big wing chair. It was that her moment of fury when she accused Pat of destroying the lithographs had been one of the few uncontrolled and unguarded moments in her life. She was quite serene now.

"I suppose Bob told you that he found out about the lithographs," she said.

"Yes."

"I doubt if he told you how."

"He suggested blackmail," Bradley said.

"What a little beast he is! He told you about the letters?"

"Yes."

She was silent for a moment, looking down at her carefully tended fingernails. "I suppose we'll have to go into that," she said. "It just happens, however, that that wasn't the method Bob used for finding out about the lithographs. He met me outside in the main hall when I left this room. He asked me what I had in the newspaper. I told him it was none of his business. He snatched the paper away from me. It was as simple as that."

Bradley had no difficulty in believing it.

"Of course, I had to explain to him then that no one was supposed to know."

"He accused you of doing the destroying," Bradley said.

Caroline shook her head as if she'd been through this sort of thing a thousand times. "He had to have some reason for telling you his little secret about the letters. He had to be important, Mr. Bradley. You'd neglected him."

"I think I understand that," Bradley said. "*Did* you destroy the pictures?"

"No, of course I didn't."

"And do you still think Pat did?"

"To be quite honest, Inspector, I'm afraid I flew off the handle about the whole business. As I think about it more calmly, I don't know."

Bradley nodded.

"I'd better explain about the letters and Bob's little blackmail racket," Caroline said. "It's not going to be easy." She drew a deep breath. "I was in love with Roger Ryan. I was always in love with him from the first time I ever saw him. That was more than thirty years ago. He came to my father's house one evening. They were associated in business. Emily and I both met him that night. I knew the minute I laid eyes on him that he was the one man in the world for me.

"Emily liked him, too. Emily and I were quite different. I was rather straightforward, direct. Emily was evasive, dainty, very female.

"Roger came to the house often after that night. He took us out separately and together. If anything, he seemed to be more interested in me. He told me all his plans, all his dreams.

"Toward the end of that summer Father took Emily and me to the seashore for two weeks. Emily had been behaving in a rather smug, self-satisfied fashion, but I was too far up in the clouds to pay much attention to her. Three days after we got to the beach I had a letter from Roger. He told me that he'd asked Emily to marry him, and that she'd accepted him. He said he'd asked her not to tell me until he could write to me. He said how fond he was of me and delighted he was that I was really to be part of his family now.

"There was nothing I could do. I told Emily how glad I was for her. She and Roger had set a date in the fall for their marriage.

"They were married and went off on their honeymoon." Caroline hesitated, then she looked straight at Bradley. "I'm going to tell you things that I've never told anyone, Mr. Bradley. I have to, in view of Bob's story. I wrote letters—three letters. That was right after I heard from Roger at the seashore. I told him how I felt. I had no shame about it. He was my man, and I didn't know any other way to fight for him.

"I think he was horrified to discover how I felt. He wrote me how sorry he was; he accepted the blame for having let me believe something that wasn't so. It really *wasn't* his fault. I had assumed things I had no right to assume. Years later he gave me back my letters. I should have destroyed them, but I didn't. Then Bob found them. He kept threatening to take them to Emily if I didn't do things he asked. There were reasons why I didn't want that. They were not reasons of my own. I didn't want Roger's life upset. . . . Which brings me to the heart of my story."

Bradley waited, his gray eyes mildly inquisitive.

"Roger and Emily went on their honeymoon," Caroline said. "About three weeks later I had a wire from Roger, asking me if I would come at once to the hotel where they were staying in the Berkshires.

"Roger met my train at Pittsfield. I'll never forget the look on his face as he came down the platform to greet me. He was pale, and he looked ten years older. I asked him if Emily was sick.

" 'God, I wish it was that simple!' he said.

"He didn't take me directly to the hotel. We walked out into the country to a shady spot beside a stream. We sat for a long time, not speaking. He—he just held onto my hand as though I were his last refuge. Finally he began to talk, slowly and hesitantly.

"What I'm going to tell you, Mr. Bradley, may not sound believable in this day and age. My mother died when Emily and I were six and four respectively. We were brought up by a succession of nurses. Our father knew very little about how to bring up girls. One thing that had been studiously avoided was any information at all about what we used to call 'the facts of life.' I had acquired this information at school. Apparently Emily had never had any curiosity about it. The result was that she had married Roger without having the slightest conception of what was expected of her as a bride.

"On their wedding night, when Roger went to her, Emily was frightened out of her life! She thought something had transformed him into a monster. She became so violently hysterical that Roger had to send for the hotel doctor. It was the beginning of a nightmare for Roger. The very sight of him drove Emily into a panic. If he so much as touched her hand she became hysterical again.

"He tried to explain to her that his behavior wasn't the result of some fantastic degeneracy peculiar to him. I believe he enlisted the help of the hotel doctor, who, belatedly, tried to make things clear to Emily. It was no use. She was in mortal terror of Roger."

Caroline paused. She lit a cigarette. "I was Roger's last hope of straightening things out. He had to get back to New York to his job. He knew Emily would probably go mad if she had to live alone with him here in this house. He begged me to come and stay with her. So I came.

"It wasn't a job I relished. But I did my level best. I talked to Emily for hours on end. I sent for our old family doctor whom she trusted. After about a month, she finally understood that Roger had done nothing that wasn't entirely normal and natural for any husband. She took hold of herself—valiantly, considering what she had been through. She tried to make it up to Roger, but I could see her cringe when he showed her any affection.

"She became pregnant almost at once. She needed me. She was terrified. But, in a way, I think she was also relieved. It meant she didn't have to deal with Roger.

"She had a very bad time when Bob was born. It was touch and go whether she would live. So I stayed on after that. I stayed on forever. Emily had Julian and Pat, and then the doctors told her she couldn't have another child. In a way, she became a semi-invalid then. Sometimes I thought it was something she'd built up in her own mind to keep her from having to fulfill her duties as a wife. The running of the house was passed on to me. She concentrated on the children."

Caroline tossed her cigarette into the fire. She looked straight at Bradley. "I don't want to pretend I didn't like being here. I still loved Roger. I couldn't have him for myself, but in a way I could share him. I preferred having the small bit of his life and his attention than all of some other man's. It was hard to keep my hands off the children. It was hard not to enter into discussion or advise about decisions. I could see that Roger had only half a life with Emily. It was bitter medicine to know that I could have supplied the half that was missing.

"Then, about a week ago, after thirty years, Roger sent for me here in the study. He was sitting where you are, Mr. Bradley." Caroline stopped, her voice suddenly unsteady.

Bradley waited.

"He began to tell me about his plan to go to Florida," Caroline said finally. "He said he knew what it would mean to me. This had been my home all my life.

" 'I've been selfish, Caroline,' he said. 'Incredibly selfish. You see, my dear, I wanted you here. I needed you.'

" 'It wasn't selfish, Roger. I've lived a very full, a very happy life.' I said.

"He leaned his head back against the chair and closed his eyes. 'There are some mistakes,' he said, 'that can't be undone. We've come to a parting of the ways now, Caroline. It's best. But it's a wrench, my dear, a severe wrench. Do you remember that day you came to Pittsfield?"

" 'I remember,' I said.

" 'When I saw you coming along the platform, Caroline, I knew I had irrevocably messed up my life.'

" 'Oh, Roger!'

" 'Is it bad to tell you now? I'm washed up, Caroline. I'm finished. I've done the very best job I could in the situation I made for myself. I've always been faithful to Emily. I've devoted every energy I had to making up to her for something that wasn't her fault or mine. And now, when I'm anchored to this chair and have no energy left, I want to be unfaithful, just once. I want to tell you, Caroline, that I've always loved you with all my heart!' "

Caroline couldn't go on. She shaded her eyes with her hand for a moment. When she looked at Bradley again, they were suspiciously bright. "That's my story, Mr. Bradley."

Bradley looked past her to the window seat where Dr. Smith had been sitting, entirely motionless, during the whole of Caroline's recital. The doctor raised his eyes now.

"How would you have handled the children differently, Caroline?" he asked.

She looked startled, as though she hadn't known he was there. "I suppose there were a dozen little things," she said.

"But, specifically, what would you have done differently?" the doctor said.

"I don't know what could have been done with Bob. Perhaps, if we had realized how bitterly he resented Julian's being born and taking over part of the spotlight, we could have handled him in such a way that the mental twist under which he's operating today wouldn't have developed."

"That's very shrewd of you," Dr. Smith said. "And Pat?"

"Pat's attachment for her father was overbalanced. She should have had more sympathy from Emily and more contact with the outside world. I might as well admit, and it sounds childish, that I saw Pat as a sort of rival of mine with Roger. I'm afraid it was all too easy for me to accuse her when I discovered those torn lithographs."

"And Julian?"

"I'm sorriest for Julian. He had a bad break in the beginning. Emily was always sick. She suffered from migraine headaches. When Julian was about four, he was screaming up and down the hall one day, playing some kind of game. The nurse came out and quieted him, because Emily was lying down. She explained why Emily was ill. It was because she'd had such a terrible time bearing children, the nurse said. She said Emily had sacrificed her health and happiness to bring Julian and the others into the world.

"It was a stupid thing to tell a child. Julian developed a feeling of guilt. He felt *he* was responsible for his mother's illness. He had to protect her; he had to make up to her for what he had done to her. Unfortunately, we never knew what the nurse had told him till years later—till after his feeling of guilt was deeply ingrained. And later, when he understood better, I think he felt that Roger, too, was guilty." . . .

After Caroline Evans had left the study, Dr. Smith spoke to Bradley from across the room.

"Extraordinary woman," he said.

"Extraordinary story," Bradley said.

"One important point, Inspector. Her perception of the three children is sound, very sound. Exactly as I see them myself. I have to believe she is almost dead-center clear on them. If that's true, her perception of the others may also be clear. Or can she be dead-right about the children and dead-wrong about Roger and Emily?"

"Since Roger and Emily, between them, pretty well wrecked her life, it isn't unreasonable to suspect she may have a very biased view of them," Bradley said.

The doctor sighed. "Of course you're right. I was trying to make it too easy for us. I'm eager to talk to Emily." . . .

Julian brought his mother into the study, protesting all the while. "This shouldn't be permitted," he fumed. "As a physician, Dr. John, I don't see how you can—"

"It's really all right, darling. I'm quite able to talk," Emily said, a little breathlessly.

Julian lowered her into the chair as if she might break into small pieces. "Can I get you a robe for your knees, Mother?"

"I'm quite all right, Julian. Really!" Her hands fluttered, slender, graceful.

"I'll stay here if you like, Mother. They can't force me to leave," Julian said.

"Julian, I'm quite able to manage. After all, these men are not ogres." Emily smiled, a little wistfully, a little tremulously, at Bradley.

"If it seems too difficult for your mother, we won't persist in questioning her, Mr. Ryan," Bradley said.

"I should hope not!" Julian said. He went out and closed the door.

Emily's hands moved vaguely, like white mist-clouds. "The others have told me something about what you've been asking," she said. "You must have a very clear idea about all of us by now. I don't know what I can add, really. We're not a very complex family."

Bradley's eyebrows went up slightly, but he didn't speak.

"All I can tell you," Emily said, "is what I've told you from the beginning—that you're wrong. Nobody murdered my husband."

"Then perhaps you can explain—"

"But surely it's quite obvious that he killed himself!" Emily said.

"What's that?" Dr. Smith said sharply. He came around to confront Emily.

"Dr. John, you knew Roger," she said. "You know how kind he was. You know that he never thought of himself first. He was always concerned with others. Surely, you can see, then, that this is what must have happened. You've heard of his idea to close the house and go to Florida? Of course, every one was willing he should go if he wanted."

Her voice floated warm and gentle through the room, vague as the movements of her hands. "But he saw what it meant to them all; a breaking up of a family which had been together through the years. I think he realized that there was only one thing he could do to prevent this. He hated being an invalid. I don't think it was any hardship for him to die. I think he did it because he thought it would be a kindness to all of us."

Bradley looked at Dr. Smith. Dr. Smith looked at Bradley.

"Did you always feel about Roger as you do now, Emily?" Dr. Smith asked. "Did you always know him to be gentle and tender?"

"No," Emily said promptly. "No, I didn't, and that is the tragedy of my life and Roger's. There was a time when I thought he was some kind of monster, brutal and savage."

"Would you tell us why you felt that way, Emily, and what changed your opinion?"

"It's not a secret," she said. "I'm surprised if Caroline didn't tell you. You see, when I married, I hadn't the faintest idea what it implied. I knew Roger as a gay and charming young man. I was very happy to marry him. But I didn't know what it meant." She looked up at the two men helplessly.

"You mean you'd had no sex education, Emily?" the doctor said.

"Yes, Dr. John. That's what I mean. Thank you. I'd had no sex education. Naturally, when Roger approached me in those terms, I thought he'd gone mad! I think I nearly died of fear. Poor Roger! He was so bewildered. He was so tender and gentle, and all the while I saw him as sinister and bestial. It was several months before I understood and could accept the idea.

"It really wasn't my fault, Dr. John. I should have been told, but you know that thirty years ago things weren't so freely talked about nor information so easily acquired."

"Once you understood things, Emily, did your relationship with Roger become completely normal?" Dr. Smith asked.

"I wish I could say it did. I wish I could have made it so. Those first few months left a mark on both of us that nothing could erase. Then there were other unfortunate factors. I nearly died when Bob was born. My health was never robust after that, as you know. These two things prevented Roger and me from ever quite having the kind of life we should have had. But don't misunderstand me, please. We were deeply fond of each other.

"But there were things I couldn't do. Roger liked to sail, and I couldn't go with him. He liked outdoor games, and I was never strong enough for them. But Roger wasn't selfish. We found things that we *could* do together. We collected lithographs, for example; lithographs of sailing ships. It wasn't so much the pictures, but the fun we had hunting them down at auction-rooms and at dealers'. Roger made a game of it, a kind of romantic game." She sighed. "I must have been a disappointment to Roger, but he never showed it. I don't think a kinder man ever lived." Her voice broke slightly at the end.

"The children were fond of him, Emily, and got along with him?"

"Surely, they've told you. I don't think they've ever had anything but love for Roger."

Bradley looked at Dr. Smith for a cue and got none. The little gray man seemed to be lost in thought. Finally he spoke: "Emily, you see, of course, how ridiculous your suggestion of suicide is?"

"But, Dr. John, it's so obvious!"

"Is it, Emily? If Roger is what you say he was and what I knew him to be, a kind and thoughtful man—if he was that why would he kill himself in such a fashion that murder would certainly be suspected? Why would he arrange it so that his family would certainly come under suspicion?"

"But, Dr. John, only the accident of your finding the water in the bottle—"

"My dear Emily, if Roger wanted to die he didn't have to empty his medicine down the drain and fill the bottle with water. *If Roger wanted to die, all he had to do was to neglect to take the medicine when he had an attack.* The substitution of the water, Emily, was the work of someone who wanted to conceal the fact that Roger hadn't gotten his medicine at the critical moment. It was the work of a murderer."

"But, Dr. John—!"

"There are only two things you can believe, Emily. Either Roger was murdered, or he killed himself with the vicious intention of dragging some other member of the family along with him into the next world! Do you believe he was such an evil and cruel man as that?"

"No!" Emily said. "No, of course I don't."

"Then you have to believe it's murder," Dr. Smith said.

She stared at him, her face white. Then she leaned forward, clinging to the arms of the chair. "I suppose I've known it all along," she said. "For God's sake, Dr. John, tell me who it is! I can't bear the waiting."

The doctor's monotonous voice suddenly had a quality of doom: "We'll tell you, Emily. Very soon, my dear." . . .

"Well, Mr. Bradley?" the doctor said.

"Well, Doctor?"

"We've heard them all." The doctor studied the toes of his polished black shoes. "If we can put the information we have together in its proper order, we should find that there is only one possible answer."

"The answer is important," Bradley said, "but I'd like to point out a troublesome little element to you. I not only have to have an answer; I must make it stand up in a court of law. That's my job."

"More difficult," the doctor said. "Much more difficult. But possible. Well, let's get at it. There is one fact I can contribute:

"You remember Lucille's saying she thought Roger had thought up this trip to Florida solely as a means of helping her to get Julian out of here and into a home of his own. This is one statement I know to be a fantasy. It was I who suggested Florida to Roger. I urged him to go there because I thought it would give him a better chance for a longer life. He wanted to live, ill health or no ill health. *He did not want to die.* This I can vouch for. Any effect that move had on the others was of secondary consideration to Roger."

"Where do we start?" Bradley asked.

The doctor sat down in the chair which the Ryan family had occupied successively. "Let us start at the beginning," he said. "Let us start with Lucille."

He leaned back and closed his eyes. . . .

It was nearly six o'clock. For five hours the study door had been closed. For five hours the various members of the Ryan family had moved quietly about the house, unnaturally quietly, knowing that behind that closed door their fate was being decided.

At five-thirty the maid brought cocktail materials into the living-room. It was a daily routine, and no one had instructed her to alter it. Bob was on hand when they arrived and promptly mixed a shakerful. A few moments later Caroline joined him. There was nothing hostile in her manner toward Bob.

"You're probably plenty sore at me," Bob said.

"Why? You haven't done anything unexpected, Bob."

"You can have back your precious letters, you know. They won't be any use to me any longer. . . . Drink?"

"Thank you," Caroline said. She looked thoughtfully at Bob, while he poured a Martini for her. "I wonder what's going to become of you, Bob?"

"I shall probably fry, as the saying goes, after the build-up my family has given me."

Lucille and Julian and Emily came into the room. Julian's hand was slipped through his mother's arm.

"There seems no reason not to go ahead with things as usual," Emily said. "Roger wouldn't have wanted us to change. You may make me a vermouth and soda, Bob." She sat down in her usual chair.

Once he was certain she was comfortable, Julian went over to the couch and sat down beside Lucille. He said he didn't want a drink.

"Where is Patricia?" Emily said.

"Sulking in her tent," Bob said.

"Caroline, won't you see if you can't persuade her to come down?" Emily asked. "Somehow, I feel we should all be together when—when the time comes."

"I'll see what I can do," Caroline said, and left them.

"I think you should know," Emily said to the others, "that Dr. John has persuaded me that Roger's death wasn't an accident. But I don't feel anger toward anyone. I think I know why it was done. I think someone could no longer bear to see Roger suffer. I think it was a sort of mistaken kindness. Of course, we will all stand together. The punishment can't be too severe when they understand why she did it."

"Hello!" Bob said. "You wouldn't be hinting that it was Caroline?"

Emily looked troubled. "I don't see how we can think anything else," she said. "You all know how fond she was of your father and how desperately unhappy his illness made her."

Julian took off his glasses and polished them. "I can't believe it of her," he said. "But I can't believe it of anyone else, either?"

There was suddenly a crowd in the doorway. Caroline and Pat were there, and so were Bradley and Dr. Smith. The room was very still as Caroline and Pat came in and sat down.

Bradley looked tired. Dr. Smith looked like Dr. Smith—neutral, unchanged, unexciting, and unexcited. He walked quietly over to a table where magazines were piled. Apparently, it was not to be his show. The Ryan family were all looking at Bradley.

"This has been a hard day for all of you," Bradley said. "It is going to be still harder before it ends, because we know, beyond a doubt, who murdered Roger Ryan."

No one spoke. No one moved. They waited for a name to form on Bradley's lips. It didn't happen just that way. He began to speak again, wearily: "This has not been a usual case. It has not been a usual investigation. We haven't been after facts in an ordinary sense. We have been searching for a point of view, an oblique perception, a fantasy perception which created a fear of Roger Ryan so strong that there was a compelling necessity for him to die. I have used the word fantasy, but you must understand that in the mind of the person who created it, it is no fantasy at all, but a stark reality. And that is a *fact*—a fact which, when we discovered it, made it unmistakably clear who the guilty person is."

Even Bob Ryan seemed to be frozen, in the act of pouring himself another drink. The slow gravity of Bradley's speech was frightening.

"Through talking to each of you we have received several varying descriptions of Roger Ryan as a person. If you were to ask me what sort of a person he was, I would probably give you a very confused answer, but I *do* know what sort of a person each of you thought he was. I *do* know that one of you feared him and saw him as a menace. It is that person who killed him."

"That's nonsense!" Julian said.

Everybody looked at him, and he polished his glasses violently. Lucille, sitting beside him, was the color of chalk.

"I wish it were nonsense, Mr. Ryan," Bradley said. "I am going to draw for all of you one of the pictures of Roger Ryan we received, and you can check it against your own perceptions.

"I have in mind the picture of a ruthless man, a man who always got what he wanted at all times, regardless of the cost to anyone else. It's the picture of a man without any real spark of love either for his wife or his children; a man who took delight in small cruelties. Worse than that, it is the picture of a man capable of enormous physical violence and brutality, a sadist. It is the picture of a man who cared nothing for the wreckage he left in his path and who, even though he was flirting with death, was still capable of creating more wreckage."

"What rot!" Caroline said calmly.

"Really, Mr. Bradley, if this is a joke—" Emily said.

"That's no more Father than I am," Julian said.

Bradley's gray eyes came to rest on Julian. "And yet that is *your* picture of him, Mr. Ryan."

Julian's jaw dropped, and he stared at the detective. "But I never said any such thing!"

"Perhaps not in those words, Mr. Ryan, but it is your story, none the less."

"Are you trying to say that I murdered Father?"

"Yes, Mr. Ryan. I am saying it."

"Julian!" It was a whisper from Lucille.

There was no color left in Julian's face, but he looked steadily at Bradley. "You're making a ghastly mistake," he said.

"Of course he's making a mistake," Emily said, her voice shaken. "It's quite ridiculous."

"Long ago, an ignorant nurse started this picture growing in your mind, Mr. Ryan," Bradley said. "She told you that your mother's illness was the direct result of bringing you and the other children into the world. You began to feel responsible; you felt guilty. You did everything you could to make up to your mother for what you imagined you'd done to her. Then, as you grew older, you began to think that perhaps it wasn't your fault. You began to see that it was your father who was responsible. It was your father who had insisted on your mother having children.

"You thought of him as cruel now, and looked for cruelty in everything he did. You saw him as thoughtless and inconsiderate of your mother, though she and everyone else says that he was the very essence of thoughtfulness and consideration. You saw him deliberately humiliating Pat, though she says she was never humiliated and that he never gave her anything but love and affection."

"Stop it!" Julian said. "You've got to listen to me!"

Bradley went on, without mercy: "With this conviction of him which you had, events took place which forced you to act. Your father announced that he was going to break up the family and take your mother to Florida. She would have to be alone with him, hundreds of miles away from the one person—you—who knew how great her danger was. You couldn't let that happen. You tried to persuade your father that it didn't make sense. He was adamant. Then there was only one thing you could do. And you did it."

Bradley stopped. No one spoke.

"You will save yourself a great deal of trouble, Mr. Ryan," Bradley said, "if you will confess to the murder."

At last Julian spoke, but not to Bradley. He spoke to Lucille, who had drawn back into the corner of the couch, white and trembling: "Darling, you've got to believe me. It's true, in a way, what he says I thought about Father. But I didn't kill him. I swear it."

Bradley walked over beside the couch. He put his hand on Julian's shoulder. "The time for talk is over, Mr. Ryan," he said. "You'll have to consider yourself under arrest."

Julian twisted out from under Bradley's hand. He stood up. "I tell you it's a mistake!" He'd gotten no help from Lucille. "Mother! Mother, you don't believe it, do you? I tell you it's a mistake."

Emily got up from her chair and went quickly to him. She put her arms around him and buried her cheeks on his shoulder. "Of course I believe you, darling. I *know* it's a mistake." She lifted her head and looked at Bradley. "I know it's a mistake," she said "because I murdered Roger."

Dr. Smith was suddenly beside Emily. He spoke very gently: "Sit down, Emily." He helped her back to her chair.

"God," Bradley said, in an undertone, "I thought for a while it wasn't going to work!"

They were like statues, all of them, even Emily. The only person who moved was Dr. Smith. He sat down on the couch beside Lucille: "Listen to me," he said. "You've got to understand. *Julian had nothing to do with this! Nothing, whatever, at all!* We never suspected him for a moment. Is that clear?"

Then Julian was on his knees beside Lucille. He dropped his face in her lap and began to sob. Lucille looked down at him, and then very slowly relaxed—relaxed, and reached out a hand to stroke his hair.

Dr. Smith got up from the couch and faced Emily. She sat very still. "That was a trick, wasn't it, Dr. John?" she said.

"Yes."

"A trick to get me to confess."

"Yes. We knew it was you, Emily. You were the only person it could be. We had to have a confession."

"You knew I'd never let Julian take my punishment."

"We knew, Emily. Not Julian. Someone else, perhaps. But not Julian."

For a fraction of a second Emily's eyes moved swiftly to Caroline, who sat beside Pat.

"You know why I did it?" Emily said.

"Yes, we know, Emily."

"I don't think you can know," she said. A strange earnestness came into her face and voice. It was as if she was suddenly caught up in some kind of religious fervor. "My husband was a master at deception, Dr. John. He deceived his own children, his friends—even so shrewd a friend as you. But I knew. I learned the truth about him the very first night we were married, when he came creeping into my room like an animal!

"He fooled everyone: Caroline, who was always infatuated with him; the doctors, who imagined that he must be as normal as any other man. They listened to his pretended bewilderment at my behavior. They left me to face him alone."

"Emily, for God's sake!" Caroline said, in a choked voice.

"I know you've always hated me, Caroline," Emily said. "You've hated me because you thought I stole your happiness. You ought to get down on your knees every night and thank God that I did! You haven't had to spend thirty years in mortal terror. You haven't had to watch your children in danger. You haven't realized that every woman who ever came under this roof was in danger!"

"Emily!"

"And I've hated you, Caroline! I've hated you because it was you who persuaded me that the fault was mine in the very beginning. You persuaded me I hadn't understood. But I had! Then I was pregnant with Bob, and it was too late." Emily looked across the room at her oldest son. "If I'd tried to leave Roger then, he'd have found some way to keep the child. A mother couldn't leave a child to a man like Roger, even to save her own life."

Pat was staring at her mother. "Mother, you don't know what you're saying!"

"Darling, I do know! I wish I didn't. Haven't I had to sit by and watch you grow into a kind of woman I would never have wanted for a daughter? I had to let you alone. It was the only way to save you from him. If you'd been less of a tomboy, more dainty, more feminine, God knows what would have happened to you.

"For years and years I have known that some day I might have to kill Roger to save myself or someone else. There was you, Caroline; there was Pat; there were dozens of other women who moved in our circle. Finally there was Lucille."

Emily's eyes turned toward her daughter-in-law, who still sat in the corner of the couch with Julian's head in her lap. "I suppose I resented you when you first came into the family, Lucille. You see, Juilan was the only person in the world who had a glimmering of truth about his father. Poor Julian! I've dreamed he might have the strength and courage to defend the rest of us from Roger.

"Yes, I resented you, Lucille. But you belonged to Julian. When I saw Roger using his charm on you, when I saw you being drawn closer and closer to him, I knew the terrible danger you were in! Julian sensed it, but he didn't really believe it. I had to act! I had to."

No one spoke, no one moved as Emily hesitated for a moment.

"It was nearly a week ago." She sounded exhausted now. "Roger had come downstairs and had called Caroline into the study."

Caroline drew in her breath sharply.

"I went upstairs and poured the medicine down the drain," Emily said. "Then I refilled the bottle with water. I knew it would only be a matter of time. I was content to wait.

"I destroyed the collection of lithographs that night. I never wanted to lay eyes on them again. Every moment spent in collecting them had been torture. I wanted no reminders.

"It wasn't murder, Dr. John!" The note of fanaticism crept back into her voice. "It was to protect myself, my family, my daughter, Julian's wife. We had risked that danger too long already!" . . .

"It's not insanity under the law," Bradley said. He and Dr. Smith and Caroline Evans were in the study.

"But it is madness!" Caroline protested. "Roger was no more a dangerous and sinister figure than I am!"

"Under the law," Bradley said, "insanity consists of being so unbalanced that you don't know what you're doing. Emily Ryan knew she was committing a murder. She is legally sane."

"But this lunacy about Roger!"

"It wasn't lunacy to her, Caroline. To her, it was quite real and beyond doubt."

"I don't understand how you were so sure. There were no real clues," Caroline said.

"There were clues in your several minds," Dr. Smith said. "Many clues. We had to find in one of you a perception of Roger Ryan calculated to produce fear and hatred of him.

"We had to couple this fear and hatred with a character of sufficient strength to act. Emily was the only person who fitted."

"But she didn't tell you how she felt! Not how she really felt!"

"No. She was in a spot. She knew you must have given us the background of her relationship with Roger. She had to admit it and she did, but she told us that she'd discovered very early in her marriage how wrong she'd been about it. She went on and on in this vein, and none of it rang true. But that wouldn't have been enough to convince us. We had the rest of you, you see.

"We knew, for example, that it wasn't Lucille. She saw Roger as kindly, as an ally, as a needed friend. She hadn't known him long enough to have any deep-seated neurotic perception of him which she might be hiding.

"We knew it wasn't Pat. We considered her, but it wouldn't stand up. Her picture of her father was completely plus, neurotically plus. We considered that Roger had done something to disillusion her. But it didn't come out anywhere. It didn't show in a single word she spoke. We had to conclude she was giving us a real picture of Roger Ryan, and, in those circumstances, she couldn't have killed him."

"And what about me?" Caroline asked.

"You might have killed him," Dr. Smith said, casually, "but you'd have done it many years ago if you'd been going to. You loved him, and you'd made up your mind to serve him as long as he needed you. You couldn't hate him, because he was ill, and you knew that I'd ordered him to Florida. He wasn't running away from you. You knew that."

Caroline's voice choked. "When I think that it was during the one and only time he ever told me he loved me that Emily was upstairs, with that bottle of medicine . . ."

"We knew it couldn't be Bob," Dr. Smith said, after a moment. "No profit in it for him. He couldn't gain money or prestige or power by Roger's dying. But Julian—ah, there was a tougher nut to crack."

"Amen!" Bradley said.

"You see," Dr. Smith said, "Julian's perception of his father was literally a reflection of Emily's. He had been subtly fed on it, first by the nurse, and then later and probably always by Emily. He came to think of his father in much the same terms that Emily thought of him.

He believed that his father was dangerous. Every element was there to make him the potential murderer. *Every element but one.*"

"And what was that?"

"Julian wasn't a doer," the doctor said slowly. "He liked to read about things and hear about them; he didn't like to do them. Julian might have dreamed of murdering his father a thousand times, but he could never have lifted a finger to do it. It was a bad trick we played on him, but it had to be done. Perhaps it will not be too bad, in the long run. Did you notice that, at the worst moment for him, he turned to Lucille? I hope that means something. Perhaps now he can operate as a man, standing on his own two feet."

Bradley struck a match and lit his pipe. "You know," he said, "I wonder what Roger Ryan was really like."

THE END